A TEXAN COMES RIDING

Matt Lonergan had given up his badge to become a cowman, to get himself a ranch somewhere and settle down. He was thoroughly sick of killing. His gun hung heavy on his hip, a weary burden. And now he was riding to pick up his cows in Goodland, a wide-open town where he'd never been before. This is where he wanted to begin his new life. But his reputation got there before him. His enemies were waiting, determined to gun him down. And he was wearing no badge. He had only his guns to protect him . . .

A TEXAN COMES RIDING

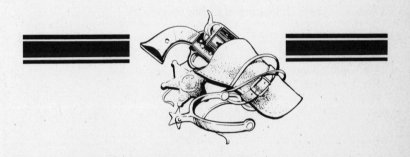

Steven C. Lawrence

ATLANTIC LARGE PRINT
Chivers Press, Bath, England.
John Curley & Associates Inc.,
South Yarmouth, Mass., USA.

Library of Congress Cataloging in Publication Data

Lawrence, Steven C.
    A Texan comes riding.

    Reprint. Originally published: Greenwich, Conn.:
Fawcett Publications, 1968.
    1. Large type books.   I. Title.
[PS3562.A916T4   1986]   813'.54   85-29388
ISBN 0-89340-952-9 (lg. print)

British Library Cataloguing in Publication Data

Lawrence, Steven C.
    A Texan comes riding.—Large print ed.
    —(Atlantic large print)
    Rn: Lawrence D. Murphy   I. Title
    II. Series
    813'.54[F]   PS3562.A916

    ISBN 0-7451-9171-1

This Large Print edition is published by Chivers Press, England, and
John Curley & Associates, Inc, U.S.A. 1986

Published by arrangement with the author

U.K. Hardback ISBN 0 7451 9171 1
U.S.A. Softback ISBN 0 89340 952 9

A TEXAN COMES RIDING

CHAPTER ONE

That Thursday morning in August, just before ten, a dusty lone rider pushed his black horse through the thick stand of willows, alders, and cottonwoods lining the Platte south of Goodland. A slight pressure of the man's wrist made the heavy-chested stallion slow and shift its weight to its forelegs. Only two people were visible at this end of the town: two young women on the back porch of an old house. Both stood when they saw the rider. Their hands quickly smoothed the low lace necklines of their dresses; they watched as if they knew exactly what the rider meant to do.

But Matt Lonergan paid no attention to the women.

A light tightening of his knees moved the black ahead a few long strides. It halted well clear of the confused clouds of mosquitoes and waterbugs buzzing along the shining white sandbars that thrust out into the sluggish, gurgling current. Then Lonergan dropped the reins to press the base of his spine. Carefully he eased forward and straightened in the stirrups so as to take the strain of his full weight off his left leg.

1

The thigh was touchy under the wide, tight bandage, but there was no real pain. Lonergan let his body relax, took off his hat, and wiped his face with his left hand. That felt fine too, no stiffness now; the fingers were as loose and nimble as they'd ever been. He started the stallion ahead again, held it to a slow walk, and angled sharp right onto the dirt road that ran parallel to the railroad. The two women frowned knowingly and turned away. They kept their backs stiff, as if they in some way possessed something of great value and had no intention of giving it to the rider.

Lonergan moved past the line of weather-aged houses and a boarded-up church, its white paint almost completely cracked off. He was a long man, bulky in his dirt-streaked white shirt and blue serge trousers that were tucked into tall boots. He sat his saddle loosely, yet somehow he looked as solid as the Civil War monument that separated the old section of Goodland from the new. His eyes helped the impression. Gray and set in smudges deepened by past pain and caution and weariness, they coolly, habitually appraised each building, each alleyway, window, and doorway while he squinted against the bright midmorning glare.

Lonergan knew the old town, and from what he'd heard, he had expected that the

2

ancient homes behind him would have been torn down. A dusty, sun-beaten town, one of a dozen that had spotted the Union Pacific's snaking length across Nebraska Territory during the year he'd ridden shotgun for the railroad—five years before he'd taken a sheriff's badge in a Texas town south of the Canadian. He thought of the Texas town now, of what he'd had and had lost there. A wild, wide-open place where the scorching winds of summer and the icy freeze of winter blew in off the Llano Estacado. A barren land of hardpan swept glass smooth, with only patches of bunch grass showing here and there—and some greasewood thickets and a few gnarled oaks. Yet, he'd had so much there, and the law he had kept was so important to both Eleanor and him.

The land ahead promised a new start. Not Goodland, though, for he knew what could come here. Beyond the town was what he'd ridden a thousand miles to have: the rich dark soil of the Platte's high north bank, where a man could live quietly and feed his cattle and grow his crops. Matt Lonergan looked past the newly erected buildings to the mile-wide river, which would always give enough water, the immense clean blue of the sky, and the good brownish-green of the prairie grass rolling and dipping and rolling again north

3

and east and west to the end of sight.

He could see a roped-off wooden bandstand built in the roadway at the town's far end, and the huge signs, long white lengths of cloth draped like black-lettered electioneering posters from the Goodland Hotel and the second story of the town hall: TRAIL END— WELCOME COWHANDS. And diagonally across Frontier on the false front of the Drovers Bar, THE TOWN IS YOURS! Lonergan's careful gaze took in the men and the women on the walks and porches, and he noted that the loading pens below the roundhouse were still empty.

The first clang of the hammer on metal startled him. Gunshots came like that. His right hand let go the leather and swept down to his holstered .44 Colt.

Then, as the hammering continued, he caught himself. While he circled wide of a group of boys playing at the mouth of an alleyway he kept the hand close to the stock of the Winchester rifle booted beneath his right knee. The blacksmith worked just inside the high open doorway of the livery, diagonally opposite the Nebraska Land and Cattle building. He didn't even glance up at Lonergan.

Lonergan knew he was letting himself get too worried; he relaxed his gun hand. One thousand miles was a long distance. The hate

4

and trouble were far behind in Adobe Wells. The life of always watching, having to be ready every minute, every second, was done. The letters he'd written buying land and ordering cattle to be picked up here had been the first step. But those long years of living by the gun had marked him worse than the scars on his arm and side and leg. He was too willing to jump at sounds and shadows.

Still, while he reined in at the land and the cattle water trough he followed each step of the man in cowhand's clothes who crossed Frontier from the saloon.

His thigh throbbed while he dismounted, slow and easy. He held his left leg stiff so as not to cause more seepage of blood. A boy's shout carried clear to him. 'Hey, it is him! See how he keeps his leg!'

'Yuh,' called another. 'Hey, Lonnie, you were right!'

They'd stopped their game. As a group, the boys jogged towards where Lonergan stood.

Lonergan pumped the trough almost full and let the black sink its nose into the cool water. He didn't pick up the dipper for himself but took off his hat and slapped the dust out of it. The cowhand's long, tanned face studied him quizzically. Two more men, both tall and wearing gunbelts, had stepped through the batwings. A third, younger, yet

5

just as tall, moved onto the saloon porch alongside them. None was a Jellison he could recognize.

'Mr. Lonergan?' the cowhand asked. He was about fifty, ten years older than Lonergan, six inches shorter. A lifetime of outside range work in all kinds of weather had sloughed off every ounce of excess flesh, leaving the leather-tough, wiry body of a cowman. He became surer now, grinned, and offered his hand. 'I'm Ted Shane. Mr. Givren sent me.'

Lonergan gripped the fingers tightly. 'I thought I'd get in early and have the paper work done before the steers come in.'

'The herd's fordin' 'bout a quarter-mile west. I've got Cox and Rourke over to the Drovers. Mr. Givren said you'd want to be started 'fore the shindig they're goin' to have.'

'I want the cows cut and trailed before dark. You can head out and meet them.' Lonergan turned away from the small faces that crowded in on him and whipped a halter knot around the hitchrail. 'I'll be out.'

'Hey, you *are* Sheriff Lonergan, aintcha?' a boy asked. He was eight or nine, shirtless, with skinny bare legs angling down from his torn knickerbockers.

'Sure he is, Lonnie,' a second argued. 'Your uncle said he'd limp from the leg them killers shot.'

'Gee, you're gonna take Mr. Telfair's place. Are you, Mr. Lonergan?'

'Go ahead, you kids,' Shane said. 'Go play and don't bother Mr. Lonergan.'

'But we need a Sheriff since Mr. Telfair quit. You gonna? Cause all them trail hands are comin' in.'

Lonergan shook his head. 'I'm a rancher now. Just that.' He pulled the Winchester from its boot and tucked it beneath his elbow. 'Let the horse drink there. Don't stand behind him.'

He caught a whispered 'Aw, gee,' and a louder 'Yuh, but he keeps his gun 'cause he knows they're huntin' him.' He slowed going up the stairs. The brown-haired boy in knickerbockers had scuttered past him to cross the porch and run ahead of him into the cattle office. He'd taken the rifle because he hadn't wanted to leave a weapon loose around children. He let it drop to his right hand and gripped the solid oak of the stock lightly, ready to pump and use. The few minutes he'd relaxed weren't reality for him. Even the children knew. Until he was sure, absolutely certain the Jellisons weren't still after him, caution was his only reality ...

'That's who he is, I tell you,' the boy was saying excitedly to the man and the woman

7

inside the office. 'He really looks like a gunfighter.'

'Whoa! Whoa, wait there, Lonnie,' the man said. He'd been working at a wide table along the far end of the large, white-painted room. The wooden scale model on the table top was of the town of Goodland, the new and old sections. There was the double line of railroad tracks, the loading pens, and the siding that stretched westward beyond the buildings almost to the Platte. The man shot a hurried glance at the dark-haired young woman behind the reception desk. But it wasn't necessary. She was already on her feet speaking to the boy.

'Your trousers, Lonnie. Look at them. You were so clean when you went out this morning.'

'C'mon, Mom. I was tellin' you.'

'I'm telling you, young man.' One fine, slim finger pointed at the door. 'March right home and put on your shirt and change those torn trousers.'

'But we were playin' ring-a-levio.'

'Lonnie Duncan.'

'Aw.' The boy backed toward the door, pouting while he watched Lonergan. 'You goin' to stay here, Mr. Lonergan?'

'Not long, son. Until the trail herd is in.'

The pout faded and Lonnie grinned. 'Then

I c'n watch you ride out. I can. I'll be back, Mom. Uncle Jimmy.'

James Hollis laughed and stepped to the front desk. 'You set up quite a stir coming in like that.' He nodded at the woman, but she wasn't smiling. She watched her son go off the porch steps and past the other boys, who were grouped around the water trough and the black stallion. 'This is my sister, Mrs. Duncan,' Hollis added. 'She handled your cattle order. And your letter to Jay Givren.'

Lonergan nodded. 'Thank you. The answer Givren sent said my land has been surveyed and all I do is sign in the Kearney bank.'

'You don't have to thank us. That's our business here,' the woman answered. She fingered through the papers she'd been filing.

'Janet,' Hollis began awkwardly, flustered. But she simply continued her work, her back held perfectly straight, thin shoulders squared; her steady eyes turned again to the window to make certain Lonnie had gone home. Hollis shook his head. There was, in his pale oval face, the suggestion of a man who spends the majority of his time inside an office, yet the effect was lost with his earnest, friendly smile.

'I asked the Givren foreman to watch for you,' he told Lonergan. 'He might be across at the saloon.'

9

'I talked to him, Mr. Hollis. I just wanted to leave my check with you before I take my cattle.'

'Oh, no. We work on commission. The check will have to be paid directly to the trail boss.' His stare flicked to the sound of bootheels on the porch. 'It will be an hour or two at the least. We keep some rooms across at the hotel for visiting cattlemen. You could have your horse fed and rubbed while you're waiting.'

The man who pushed past the screen door was heavy-set, graying, and extremely neat and clean in his tailored brown broadcloth. Once inside, he took off his expensive Stetson and mopped the round of his jawline and neck with a handkerchief. He nodded at Hollis and Janet Duncan, offered his free hand genially to Lonergan.

'I'm Herbert Rollins,' he said as cordially. 'Those kids certainly let it be known you're here. When Hollis accepted your cattle order, he mentioned our company's shipping policy.'

'I plan to drive my own herd, Mr. Rollins. I can get used to them better that way. And have a good look at what I've bought.'

'Well, of course. We want every cattle rancher to know everything we've planned for this town.' He gestured at the scale model of Goodland. 'When it comes time to ship your

10

beef, we want you to remember our facilities.'
He laughed good-naturedly. 'You'll have time
to oversee what we can do when Frontier
really opens up for the cattle crew.'

'I've seen trail towns. Enough of them. I'm
starting my herd west soon as they're cut and
paid for.'

'Oh, but I thought...' Irritated, his gaze
rested on Hollis momentarily, then returned
to Lonergan. 'We have the room to hold your
cattle the few days. We offered a good price
for such a short time as sheriff.'

'I wrote I didn't want the job. Not for three
days or three hours, Mr. Rollins.' He touched
his hat brim and moved to leave.

The fingers of the hand that held the
handkerchief brushed Lonergan's sleeve, and
he paused. Rollins had drawn a silver-
wrapped cigar from his inside coat pocket, but
he thought better of offering it.

'We knew Telfair was getting through
before this first trail crew pays off. Lonergan,
we're building to be the biggest cattle town in
this country. We were depending on you.'

'Not on me, Mr. Rollins. I had enough of
using a gun when I took off my badge. I'm
interested only in ranching. You want to have
a wide-open town for cattle crews, that's your
business. I'll come in to ship beef, but that's
all I want of what you're doing.'

11

Rollins' tone changed then and became almost a threat. 'The Town Council thought you'd want this. The way the Jellisons shot you up in that last gunfight. You'll need good friends if the rest of that family comes after you.'

Lonergan looked directly into Rollins' eyes and included James Hollis and his sister in his answer.

'If the Jellisons, or anyone else from that life, do come,' he said calmly, 'my good friends are the last ones I'll want to stand with me.' He swung around and limped out of the office.

*   *   *

Lonergan stepped into clear view of the three men standing at the window of the Drovers Bar. Bol and Lew Jellison, both tall and in their mid-forties, didn't move; they simply watched Lonergan halt at the water trough and water his black. Bol's son, Rob, as tall and stringy as his father and uncle, didn't have their patience. He edged near the half-frosted saloon window and followed Lonergan's every step as he led the stallion away from the crowd of boys. There was a wide, squat shadow in front of the land and cattle building. Heat shimmered from the saddle and bridle metal

12

and from the silver plate on Lonergan's rifle. White glare reflected from windows behind Lonergan, giving him less chance the way he'd have to face the sun.

'We hit him now,' Rob said. 'Soon as he gets clear of the kids.' He started toward the batwings.

'Hold it,' his father called. His hat, pulled low over his eyes to shade the glare, made his face square, stone-blocked, the skin stretched tight along his jaw and nose and mouth. 'Not yet, Rob. He's goin' into the livery.'

'He'll never be easier to bust. Right in the sun.'

'We don't know. If he took that badge, he's the law here. We can't cut him down in the open if he is. You heard Rollins say he was goin' to offer him the job.'

Rob muttered disagreement, yet he remained as he was.

Bol Jellison switched his gaze. The town's backside, where they'd left their mounts, was clear. The crossroads leading north, lined on both sides by the new two-story, white-painted homes of the get-rich-quick business thumpers, were as wide open. But he couldn't be positive. Shane and Givren's two other cattlehands were out of sight beyond the bandstand at Goodland's west end. They wouldn't interfere. Still, they couldn't go after

Lonergan yet. Their fight was with a man who didn't wear a sheriff's badge. Throw down on a tin star in the middle of a town and you brought too much trouble.

'He's turnin', lookin' at the river,' Rob said. 'Nothin' I c'n see on his shirt, Paw.'

'No, I said. Dangit, you hold right here.'

'Your paw's right,' Lew Jellison put in. 'We'll get him. Don't you worry none. At our own good time.' His square face pressed close to the glass. 'That loudmouth's comin' back.'

Bol nodded. He'd watched Rollins leave the cattle office. Rob was right about the edge they'd have. The silver wrapping that Rollins was unwinding from a cigar sparkled in the sun's brightness, the same sun Lonergan would have to shoot into. They'd ridden a thousand miles, had hunted for Lonergan every inch of the distance, but he'd been too smart to get caught in the open. Two more Jellisons had signed on with the trail drive that included Lonergan's five hundred cattle in case Lonergan had tried to meet the Texans and cut his herd early.

Lonergan hadn't gone close to the drive. That didn't surprise Bol. The man had been tough enough and clever enough to face three Jellisons down in Adobe Wells and last through it with no more than a shot-up arm and leg. He'd known enough to get out of the

14

Amarillo hospital before Bol was told about his brother and his two nephews and had time to collect the rest of the family. But they would all be here. The one thing they had was time.

'Don't let Rollins see you watching,' Bol said.

'Paw, Lonergan'll walk right out of that livery.'

'You look inside, Rob.' He unhooked his bootheel from the brass rail and swung around at the counter. 'Dobie, another setup.'

The bartender left the two saloon girls he'd been speaking to opposite the long gilded mirror. The backbar and the walls were decorated with animal heads, antlers, and the rigid wings of birds that could be hunted along this plains country. He hesitated below a buffalo head and chose a cheap red whiskey from the line of bottles.

'You're plannin' on bein' around,' he said while he poured, 'better take our rooms upstairs now.'

'We're not stayin',' Bol said.

The bartender ran his hand through his thick black hair. He allowed his glance to slide to the women, a brunette and a bosomy blonde, who watched them talk. 'Anythin' you want, get early, boys.' He rolled up one of the elastic garters on the sleeve of his collarless

15

white shirt and grinned knowingly. 'There's goin' to be a real time in this town, and you can start early.'

Bol Jellison took his shot glass. 'Leave the bottle.' He laid a five on the counter.

Dobie shrugged his shoulders. 'Every man to himself. I say you're really missin' somethin'.' He moved again toward mid-bar to meet Herbert Rollins coming past the swinging doors.

Rob Jellison said, 'Lonergan's headed into the hotel.'

'Shut,' Bol ordered. 'Can't you hold down?' He caught his son's tense stance and watched Rollins halt opposite Dobie and shake his head to the bartender's first question.

'No, he's interested only in his damn cattle,' the Jellisons could hear the heavyset cattle agent say. 'Loomis will have to keep the control by himself.'

Rob said, 'Paw? There's no badge to stop us.'

Lew Jellison downed his liquor in one swallow. 'He'll be alone in the hotel,' he said. 'We c'n do it 'fore Dave and Sid get in.'

'Dammit, Paw,' Rob blurted. 'He's caught in there. We cover both front and back doors.' He waited, poised, his right hand rubbing at the butt of his Colt. Then, quickly, he stepped toward the batwings. 'Uncle Dan was my kin.

And my two cousins.'

Bol reached out to stop him. 'No, not like this.' But Rob was gone outside.

Bol Jellison was moving, hurrying fast alongside Lew. 'Cut down the alley and take the back. That fool kid. He won't stand a chance unless he's shootin' when he goes into that lobby.'

CHAPTER TWO

Inside the hotel lobby Matt Lonergan was watchful, concerned. The idea to come in early and get his business done without anyone knowing he was here was completely dead. Only a few days and he would be on his own, working his hundred acres, and maybe in a year or two nobody would remember where he'd gone. Often enough in his long ride he'd pictured himself gee-hawing a pair of mules behind a breaking plow and settling down each night in his own home after a good hard day. Only Eleanor was missing. He missed her more and more the closer he'd come to it these last few weeks.

Children had followed him from the livery, mainly the smaller boys who'd crowded around the water trough. They waited beyond the porch, kicked the dust of the street, and talked loud enough for him to hear their clatter. It wouldn't be long before they'd crowd around the outside door, pressing their noses and foreheads against the screening, and get in the way. Lonergan laid the Winchester flat on the registration desk and tapped the small, round counter bell. A stale odor of fried bacon and eggs lingered in the comparatively cool air of the room. Placed neatly about the carpetless floor were a battered cowhide divan and four cane-backed chairs, all spread enough to allow plenty of free movement.

Somewhere outside, beyond the rear door, voices sounded. Lonergan hit the bell again, this time banging it so the jingle echoed hollowly up along the second floor staircase.

The back door swung in, and two men carrying cases of whiskey bottles stepped into the lobby. The one in the lead was fiftyish, wide-shouldered, with thinning gray hair combed to cover a bald spot. The bones of his arms were long and muscled; and those of his wrists, knobby and red. He strained under the heavy weight. He broke into a grin when he saw Lonergan.

'Just a minute. Only a minute,' he said. He set both cases down on the bottom of the staircase and added across his shoulder to the young redhead behind him, 'Put them in the

18

storeroom, Alfred. No, lock the door before you do.'

The grin held while he halted behind the counter and flicked open the register. 'I just don't want any of those girls from Dobie's being sneaked in. I'm willing to supply liquor, but that's all I want.'

'I was told by Mr. Hollis you have rooms reserved for his company.'

'Certainly.' He watched while Lonergan signed, then stared at the inked name. He looked up and smiled wider. 'There's plenty water for a bath. I'll have Alfred...' His mouth didn't change with the sudden gasp. 'No! No!'

Lonergan had heard the swish of the porch door as it opened. His hand streaked for his gun as he whirled; the words of the hotelman and the shocked outbreak of shouts from the children were muffled under a man's loud voice.

'This is for the Jellisons, Lonergan!'

Gunfire blasted through the lobby, two shots that sounded almost as one. Lonergan's hat was torn from his head. The thin crouching man who'd come in shooting was stiffened by the impact of Lonergan's bullet. He jerked around, dropping his sixgun, and was slammed viciously against the wooden doorframe.

The hotelman started for the porch. His handyman knocked over a whiskey case and sent the liquor bottles rolling across the pine floor.

'Don't go near him,' Lonergan ordered. He moved fast, and reached the dropped Colt. Someone in the back yard shook the rear door and yanked at the knob, but the lock held. Lonergan's sixgun barrel didn't leave the downed man or the open porch doorway while he picked up the weapon.

The gunman was young; couldn't be more than twenty. He groaned, fought back tears of pain and frustration, and pressed at his bloody right shoulder.

'Stand,' Lonergan told him. 'Quick, you stand.'

'He's hit bad,' the hotelman said. Watching helplessly, he added, 'You crazy fool. Don't you know who this is? Don't you?'

'Clear the boys away,' Lonergan said. Men had appeared behind the children, and they moved in close on the steps. Louder shouts sounded along the street. Thumps of boots kicked on the boardwalks. Lonergan didn't shift the silver barrel, but kept it directly on the men he could see.

'You fool,' the hotelman repeated. 'You know who?'

'I know,' Rob Jellison snarled. His teeth
20

bitten together, he pulled himself erect. His eyes searched the converging crowd of faces and stared hard at the men shoving in from the rear. Leaning against the wall, he spat. 'I'm a Jellison, Lonergan! I damn well know you!'

'You shouldn't have tried. It's not worth this.'

'It is. I come all the way after you.' Pain made him flinch, but he controlled that. 'All alone, Lonergan. I wanted you for myself!'

Muttering and movement broke out, and women's voices mixed in the crowd that grew on the porch. A mother called her son's name; another spoke sharp words to her husband for moving in so near the trouble.

'You wouldn't come all this distance alone,' Lonergan said. 'Listen.'

'Hell with what you want. I didn't get you, one of us will. This isn't the end. Not by a damn sight it isn't.' He coughed and tightened his hand. Blood seeped through the clenched fingers.

'Let me by here. C'mon, open up.' A stubby, round-faced man wearing a sheriff deputy's badge on his checkered shirt came through the onlookers. He was in his late twenties, and there was a harsh leanness to his body. He stared from the weapon in Lonergan's hand to Rob Jellison. 'Who

21

started that?'

'This one,' the hotelman said, pointing at Rob. 'He come in here with a gun in his hand.'

'You saw it, Mr. Lowney?'

'I was at the desk and I could see him shove the screen door open.' He motioned wildly at his handyman and Lonergan. 'Alfred Park was in here, too. He'll tell you Lonergan was only talking to me.'

'He was. That's right,' the handyman said. 'I saw from the back door.'

'Take him in then,' a voice called from the crowd. 'You're the law here.'

'Yes, dammit, Loomis,' a second added. 'Clean this up 'fore the trail crew gets in. We don't want trouble hangin' over us.'

Loomis took hold of Rob Jellison's shoulder. Wobbly on his feet from loss of blood, Rob staggered. One town man, then another, moved in close to help the wounded man walk.

Lonergan followed into the doorway. He knew by the way Jellison had to be supported that he was hurt worse than he showed. The town was exactly as he knew it would be after a gunfight: the watchers gathered in so tight and thick that they bellied out clear to the opposite walk. Boys who hadn't been grabbed and herded off by their mothers and fathers ran along behind the deputy and his prisoner, excited and fascinated by what they watched.

One woman who waited at the porch edge for the crowd to dissolve touched Lonergan's arm and stared into his eyes. Her face was scared, questioning. 'Why? Why here? Why in our town?' she asked shrilly. 'We've never had shooting here.'

Without answering, Lonergan turned into the lobby. Lowney and his handyman were bringing a bucket of soapy water from the kitchen to scrub clean where Rob Jellison had fallen and bled.

'The water will be up for you,' Lowney said. 'Soon as Alfred's through with this.'

'I'll use the basin,' Lonergan told him. 'I'll be in just until I rest and get the dust off.'

'Why? Look, Mr. Lonergan, that wasn't your fault. I saw it. You had to shoot.'

Lonergan nodded slowly. 'I had to,' he said, 'but I can't help thinking what it would be like if I'd missed and hit one of those kids.'

CHAPTER THREE

A knock on the door made Lonergan move to the chair where he'd draped his gunbelt. Holding the large, soggy towel with his left hand, he drew the .44 Colt with his right.

'Mr. Lonergan?' The knocks banged again, quicker. 'Mr. Lonergan, it's Al Park. I've got more hot water.'

Lonergan turned the key in the lock and opened the door. 'I won't need any more, thanks,' he said. 'I'm about through.'

Alfred Park's long, bony face stared at the pink welts on Lonergan's shirtless left arm and the jagged scar of an almost faded wound that ran the length of his ribs on the right side.

'Well, Mr. Lowney thought you'd need it. I'll tell him you're checkin' out.' He quieted a moment, and during the silence the far-off noise of cattle being driven came through the open window. The bawling was clear in the windless air, and a lowing, like distant little horns. 'The livery delivered your horse. I tied him out front.'

'I appreciate that. The back door is still locked?'

The mop of thick red hair nodded. Alfred's eyes unconsciously flicked across the healed wounds again.

'Thank you, Al,' said Lonergan. 'I'll be down.'

He closed the door and slid the Colt into its holster before he dropped the towel into the soapy water of the basin. He shook his head while he put on his shirt. Ten years he'd planned to get to this town. He and Eleanor had saved and planned, but not for this. You can scrimp and go without and save every cent possible from four thousand a year, believing you could build up security. Then, finally, you'd move to where you and your wife would have your own home and land. Only you never thought the everlasting heat and dusty dry climate would get into a woman's lungs so bad. After all the troubles and privations, that she'd never live to enjoy it. And because you'd been hit so hard by that, you became careless and gave a family of cattle thieves their chance to almost finish you.

He remembered the day he'd gotten the Jellisons a mile south of the Canadian. He never had figured why they'd taken every last steer from their closest neighbor. Less than fifty head of cattle. Dan Jellison and his sons had run them straight for their own spread and hadn't even bothered to change the brands. He'd been alone when he'd found their tracks and had tried to talk to them when he'd caught up. Dan had started to shoot. Then his sons. Dan and one of the sons had died before Lonergan had dropped from his own horse with two bullet holes in him. The second son, hit bad, had tried to get away on foot past the stampeding cattle they'd stolen.

Lonergan remembered the people of Adobe

Wells when he'd brought them in, how some had lifted the saddle blanket he'd thrown over the son caught in the stampede. Old Grandfather Jellison had never stopped in at the hospital to see him. He didn't even know what the grandfather looked like, or the rest of the Jellisons. The old man had simply made his statement at the burial that the family would take care of its own. Thinking of that, Lonergan buckled the gunbelt and adjusted its hang. He had believed he was through depending on the weapon. He had hoped.

But the heavy sixgun in the holster lying flat against his right thigh was exactly what it had been: an integral thing in his existence, a natural appendage, to be cleaned and tended and carried like an extra arm or leg or eye, always ready to come out and up. He wanted to think of Eleanor, to find some help in the countless hours they'd talked and planned, to know in some deeply personal way she was still with him. The sight of Jellison in the doorway and the boys' small faces pressed into the screen behind him were too fresh in his memory. His senses were honed down to the bare necessity to kill or be killed.

Instinctively, his flesh braced itself when he turned the knob and pulled open the door. He watched the hallway and the line of closed doors, waiting, suspicious, ready.

The tightness of flesh and nerves, the watchfulness and readiness—all were still there in his walk across Frontier and into the jail.

James Hollis stood with the deputy inside the sheriff's office. The pair glanced around quickly at the click of Lonergan's bootheels. Beyond them in the cell block, a black-suited doctor worked over Rob Jellison. The odor of carbolic acid was strong in the room. It killed any trace of the smell of the trail herd that had become so strong in the street. The thick, unpainted stone walls of the jail muted the sound of the cattle and the yells and shouts of the trail crew driving the point Longhorns into the loading pens.

Hollis' worried features turned hopeful. 'You decided to think over that offer, Mr. Lonergan?'

'I'd like to talk to him,' Lonergan answered, staring at the man lying on the cell bunk. Rob Jellison hadn't moved; he just stayed quiet, and lines of pain cut deep and pale at the edges of his mouth.

'He's lost a great deal of blood,' Hollis said. He watched the deputy nod. 'Loomis and I were wishing.'

Loomis said, 'I expected you'd take over temporary. I was only deputy for Telfair when he quit 'cause he didn't want anythin' of a trail town.' He wiped his mouth with the back of his hand. 'I haven't had experience handlin' a Texas trail crew.'

'It's your job,' Lonergan said. 'First thing you do is put on the sheriff's star. Stand up behind it; they'll do what you say.' He moved closer to the vertical bars. 'Doctor, can he talk?'

The doctor didn't answer. He was well along in years, a skeleton of a man with the juices of life dried in him. Yet his wrinkled hands moved just as deftly as a much younger man's while he probed for pieces of shirt that had been shredded in the bloody wound.

'Doctor?'

The doctor looked across his shoulder. 'You wait. Can't you see how bad he is with a vein cut? You come into a town and start your gunfights. You think you can do exactly what you want?'

'Lonergan didn't start it,' said Hollis. 'Doctor Kanter, he just wants to speak to him.'

'No fight would've happened if the pens weren't built,' the doctor snapped. 'The town was going along fine as it was. I want him to know everybody in Goodland didn't ask for

28

the likes of him comin' here.'

Rob Jellison's eyes fluttered and opened. He breathed heavily, wheezing. 'Get rid of him, Doc.'

'Only a minute, Doctor,' Lonergan asked. He went on to Jellison. 'I didn't want a shootout. I could have put that bullet somewhere else. I'd rather have you see how foolish it is.'

'Won't be foolish. Not when my kin gets to you. My family.'

'Your family is wrong. If there are more, I want to know.'

'You'll know. You'll see, mister. Doc.' He coughed and his whole face paled. 'I want him out, Doc.'

The doctor pressed the ugly, swelling wound to halt the flow of blood even the slight movement had caused. 'Loomis, get him out of here. Lock the door out there so I won't be bothered again.'

Lonergan saw Loomis nod, but that was all the deputy did. Lonergan stepped past Hollis and the lawman, then moved outside onto the walk.

He'd tried. He had tried. If Jellison hadn't come alone, the others would know. Lonergan quickened his stride once off the walk, flexed his fingers, and wiped the warm, sticky sweat from his palm. They'd come, maybe now,

29

surely when they learned how hard a time the doctor was having with the bleeding. Lonergan had almost begged to be left alone. To be allowed to look forward, and still to look back with all his mind and heart. He dreaded even the short walk to the cattle pens. Watching, waiting, his mind and gunhand itching to get more trouble over with. It was as if all his hope had pinched down and run dry.

'Hey, Mr. Lonergan. Wait, Mr. Lonergan!'

His hand had dropped. He hooked his fingers into the belt over the solid metal of the .44 cartridges and paused for Lonnie Duncan to reach him.

'You goin' to ride out now, Mr. Lonergan?' The boy's wide-eyed stare swept the railroad and loading area and the hundreds of milling, tight-packed Longhorns already in the pens. 'The train'll be comin' soon. They're goin' to take pictures. Boy-oh-boy, this is somethin'!'

'I'll see you, Lonnie,' said Lonergan. 'Stay back here 'til I'm gone. Keep on the walk in case a few steers are chased through town.'

The boy's grin widened. 'Yuh, I heard about that. Some cowhands drive them onto porches. They do that with their horses, too.'

'Lonnie.'

Lonergan and the boy faced Janet Duncan. She was out of breath, hurrying from the land and cattle building. She was very concerned;

her soft, flushed skin looked clean and bright in the sunlight, and she was very lovely. She held herself handsomely, but her worry and resentment weren't kept hidden from Lonergan.

'Go into Uncle's office,' she said. 'Lonnie.'

'Mom, the kids are goin' to watch the loadin'.'

'Into the office.' Her stare appraised Lonergan deliberately. 'You shouldn't be with him after your trouble. You know that.'

'Mrs. Duncan, I want him off the street. No child should be out in these streets.'

The loud, wild, rebel yell that pierced the town's stillness shut off any answer she might give. Six members of the trail crew who'd finished penning the point Texas cattle had broken from the herd to gallop in ahead of the rest for a first drink. More shouts followed. The fast-moving horses kicked up clouds of dust and chunks of brownish clod while the cowhands waved their shapeless hats crazily and called towards the women on the Drovers' second floor railed porch.

Lonnie Duncan scurried onto the walk beside his mother. Janet pressed him close and watched the lead rider sweep past the bandstand into the edge of the business district. He was a long, thin man, whiskered like the others. He kept his powerfully muscled steeldust running hard right to the saloon hitchrails. Jerking his mount to a stop, he called around to those behind him. All gave out yells and laughed as the tall man scaled his sombrero ahead of him so it scuffed the dirt and rolled on its rim and bounced under the kicking hoofs. Both free hands waved at the saloon girls in an overdone, lewd gesture.

Janet's head shook. 'This isn't what we wanted,' she said. 'Not what any of us really wanted.'

She'd lost her straight ladylike stance and was only a terribly frightened mother getting her child in off the street. She didn't even glance back at Lonergan while she moved up the porch steps and into the safety of the building.

CHAPTER FOUR

Bol Jellison stood inside the Drovers' batwings and watched the six cattle-hands tie their horses. His two brothers who'd made the long drive were there. They'd seen Lew and him. Bol listened to the laughter and talk and the catcalls they gave the saloon girls, and the low, expectant conversation behind him. Dobie had a full line of whiskey bottles out

32

and ready. The women were just as ready along the counter and at the tables; two were in the open doorways of the second floor, prepared and waiting.

'Lonergan's nice and clear,' Lew said beside him. One hand strained against the doorslats. The fingers of the other gripped the bone handle of his sixgun. 'Dave and Sid'll be ready soon as they reach us.'

'No. No, let them in. I want to tell them.'

'Dammit, he'd be in a pine box if you'd listened to Rob. No back door'll be locked this time.'

'No. Not with Rob so bad in there. Not yet, Lew.'

Bol pulled the swinging door in for the six to step past. Lonergan had purposely walked slow to let the riders enter first. He'd kept to the middle of Frontier, clear of the other people who'd come into the street. A line of black train smoke showed far out on the flat to the east, the puffs getting larger while Bol looked. The excitement had gone through the whole town, with most of the men converging on the saloon. The women and children came off their house porches and lawns and headed for the bandstand to wait for the celebration to get started.

The tall whiskered trail boss stepped inside first. 'Wal, damn me,' he said around to the rest. 'Damned if we ain't got a find here.'

'Man, Chingo'll have something to say you didn't bring him in,' the man directly behind said. Laughter broke out from the cowhands and along the bar.

Dobie waved a whiskey bottle that barely missed Herbert Rollins' head. 'Come on, Texans! First drink's on the house!'

Bol forgot the shouts and remarks made about the waiting women. Dave and Sid lagged after the other four men and dropped off alongside him.

'We heard,' Dave said. 'Them railroaders told us Rob's still bleedin' bad.' Dave was an inch shorter than Bol, older by two years, his face as square and stone-blocked under three months' growth of beard. Sid Jellison, the youngest of the brothers and the thinnest, glanced up and down the town's center street with a sneer that twisted his pencil-line mustache. 'He still locked in there?'

Nodding, Bol started to answer. Lew said quickly, 'Lonergan's the big one wearin' the blue suit. We could bust him and have Rob out in no time. The law's so pussy-foot.'

'I said we don't.' Bol grabbed Lew's sleeve and jerked him toward the bar corner. He looked over his shoulder at Dave and Sid. 'Rob can't be moved. We don't push them into anythin' like that.'

Lew swore. 'We come here to get Lonergan. Grandpaw...'

'Grandpaw didn't figure on Rob gettin' shot.' Bol stared at his other two brothers and noticed how Dave watched the crowd that had formed opposite the back-bar mirror. 'Lonergan'll keep.'

Dave nodded. 'He's goin' out after his stock. That Givren foreman talked to Kling.' And when Lew began to sputter, a wave of one hand quieted him. 'We come for the cows, too. Me and Sid didn't drive that herd all this time for just waitin' on Lonergan's showin' up.'

'We figured they're ours,' Sid agreed. 'We kill Lonergan, we get his five hundred head. We wait 'til he pays Kling. They all think our name's Johnson. It'll be outside town, and it won't be connected to Robby.'

'He's got only three riders with him,' said Dave. 'It'll be easy.'

Bol didn't move. Lew sniffed and spoke. 'Okay, we wait 'til he drives his cows.' More town men had pushed into the saloon to add to the noise and talk along the bar. He nodded to where Herbert Rollins tried to hold the movement and confusion down so he could speak to the trail boss. 'We got time,' Lew went on. 'No sense to miss this.'

Dave and Sid Jellison headed toward the
35

crowd of drinkers. When Bol didn't follow them, Lew hesitated. 'Bol?'

'I'll be with you,' Bol said. He stared through the top half of the frosted window, following each step Lonergan took coming onto the porch. 'I just want to be sure. Damned sure what he's going to do.'

★　　★　　★

Lonergan slowed his stride even more at the blast of the train whistle; the sound was loud and shrill in the blistering-hot noon air. Boys who'd gathered at the hitch-rails left the horses to head for the loading pens to watch the cattle cars backed into position. The crowd at the bandstand grew each minute; but the groups were quiet and restrained. Those beyond the high wooden platform edged aside a little to keep clear of four to five hundred rangy, sunburned, and toughened Longhorns that members of the cattle crew drove in close to the bandstand. Women and girls watching the smaller children nearer the business district stared around at their husbands and fathers on the saloon steps. Lonergan made his way past the older, married men, who had remained on the porch or stopped immediately outside the batwings.

Inside, the younger single men of the town

and the few punchers off the local ranches who'd ridden in for a big time were more reluctant to give space. Packed tight right to the counter, their high-crowned hats and tobacco smoke clouded the light thrown by the shaded, hanging lamps. Lonergan pushed through to the bar, pausing while one or another resisted his passage momentarily; he then eased away as men gave him sidelong stares and scowls and faint nods to quick spoken words of a neighbor.

'. . . and it is because of what you are doing for Goodland,' Rollins was saying. 'We've made a new town. We built the stock pens and offered a higher price for cattle because we believe in our town. We believe our fine state will someday . . .'

'Oh, blow it, Rollins,' the bartender said roughly. 'Can't you see these men want to drink? And enjoy themselves?' He scanned the deeply tanned, sweating faces opposite him. 'We did more than build a new town for you cattlemen. You c'n see what else we've got that's built exactly right.'

A loud guffaw came from the trail boss Rollins had been addressing. More laughter erupted—rough, knowing, male laughs and some womanish giggles. Lonergan edged in behind the trail hands and saw the irritated gesture the bartender gave dismissing Rollins.

'Go ahead,' Dobie said. 'Save your speeches for later. Let them enjoy themselves.'

'Look here, Jonas. I only wanted to show our appreciation.'

'Do it at your celebration outside then. They'll be out soon enough.' He leaned across the polished mahogany and spoke to the punchers. 'You ready for another one, Mr. Kling?'

The tall, angular trail boss was about forty; he grinned as he set down his glass. 'I'm 'bout ready for a lot of things I ain't had in a spell,' he said. The woman beside him, a bosomy blonde in a deep-cut yellow dress, smiled and circled her arm across his shoulders. He laughed with her and swung around to face Rollins. His faded blue work shirt and jeans were stained with the sweat and the dirt of the cattle drive. He wore an ivory-handled Starr .45 low on his right hip. His high-heeled boots were old and dusty, and his long whiskered jaw jutted out below a twisted-brimmed sombrero that was as much a part of him as the thick black hair that showed under it and along his ears and neck. 'You, Rollins. That train was supposed to be waitin'.'

Rollins fingered his cigar. 'I'm sorry about that. It was due an hour ago. I had everything ready. We were going to have pictures taken and . . .'

38

'You get that train in. We'll be out to load.'

'It's coming now, Mr. Kling. If you'll all step out to the bandstand where your cows are waiting.'

'We'll be out,' Kling repeated. His nod took in the puncher nearest him, as thin and whiskered and leathery as himself, wearing a big Texas hat and a gunbelt over his tight denim trousers. 'Dave Johnson'll see to it.'

'But we need you, Mr. Kling. You and your whole trail crew.'

''Kay. Okay, but don't bother us 'til then. We're goin' to be busy.'

Rollins' hurried, 'I won't. Thank you, Mr. Kling,' was almost lost to Lonergan in the outbreak of talk and laughter among the cowhands and the saloon women. Kling had turned to the blonde and his refilled shot glass. Circling his left arm around the girl's middle, he hugged her to him and raised the whiskey. 'Here's to it,' he told the others. 'Hurry up now.'

Lonergan halted behind Kling, said, 'You did a good job bringing that herd in. Right on time.'

'What?' Kling stared at him, the question in the deep weather lines of his face. 'You're not with the cattle office?'

Lonergan shook his head and offered his hand. 'My name's Lonergan. Those were my five hundred head of Longhorns you brought up from Midland. I'll go out and take them now if they're ready.'

'He's the one who threw down on that kid,' said the thin leathery cowhand beside Kling. One hand brushed the blonde back from between himself and the trail boss. The fingers of his right toyed with the small shot glass. Eyes narrowed, he stared directly into Lonergan's face, his long body as tense as a stretched bow. 'He was a boy from the Llano, Chet.'

Kling hadn't taken Lonergan's hand. 'You know we lost three days pickin' up them cows.' He was as aware as Lonergan of the attitude along the bar, the under-current of low talk among the town men, and the calm anger in Dave Johnson's words. When Lonergan drew a bank check from his shirt pocket, the trail boss wouldn't accept it. 'Not 'til after delivery. We lost ten head crossin' the Republican. We'll have to settle that.'

'My payment is for cattle delivered at this railhead.'

Chet Kling pushed away the check. 'I'll be out 'fore that politician spouts his speechin'. I'll settle then.'

Dave said, 'I don't like the smell, Chet. We give him his cows, he'll take off. That'll suit me.'

'Me, too,' Sid said in a low voice. He'd stepped away from the brass rail and stalked to a spot on the left of Lonergan. The crowd edged out and flowed clear of the bar's middle to make an arena.

Kling laughed loudly. 'You boys want fun?' He watched the ring of faces and saw how the bartender nervously poured a glass of whiskey.

'No, please, Mr. Kling,' the bartender said. 'Not in here. I've set everything up for you. We're givin' you so much.'

Lonergan glanced to the left and right, and caught how a third cowhand, bottle in hand, sauntered around him. His eyes showed nothing, but missed nothing. Here and there a man grinned expectantly. The saloon girls' worry and fear could have been painted on.

'Please,' Dobie asked again. 'He's leavin'. He said he was. Look, he'll be outside my place. He'll be outside town.'

'He's right,' the bosomy blonde said. 'You wreck this bar, you'll miss more than whiskey. We wouldn't want that.'

Chuckles came then—low, held-down, overanxious sounds that died when Dave raised his hand. 'I figure you'll get yours, Lonergan. You're not worth the spoilin's.'

'Get goin',' said Sid. 'You know when you're lucky. You better know.'

Dobie waved at the men between Lonergan and the porch. 'Let him through there. Come on you, open up.'

The low chuckles grew and blossomed into laughter and loud-spoken, snide remarks. 'Chet, we'll go get that speech makin' over with,' Sid said, watching Lonergan turn. 'He's bein' chased out, let him have his cows so he c'n run quick.'

'Yeah,' Dave added. 'He wants to draw on someone his equal, he'll be outside town limits. He'll get every bit of his.'

Kling was laughing now, wild guffaws joined by a complete outbreak of shouts and catcalls that followed Lonergan past the swinging doors. It had been well done, the calm taunts of the cowhands making him seem ridiculous, not worth their trouble of fighting him here and now. Matt Lonergan saw the doubt on the faces of those who'd listened from the porch and caught the feeling and attitude that had seeped like smoke on the wind from inside. A yell could come, a shouted challenge that would force all this to the one climax he didn't want.

★　　★　　★

At the far end of Depot Street the train ground to a stop. The thick smoke that poured from its squat, barrel-like stack partially obscured its coal car and long line of cattle cars. James Hollis and two more town men waited on the platform and greeted the passengers who stepped off. Lonergan reached his stallion and moved close to the hitchrail to undo the granny knot Alfred Park had used to tie the animal. Two men carrying long black cases came down Depot with Hollis. Link-and-pin coupling clanged, brake chains squeaked, and the engine chuffed, billowing black cinder-smelling smoke while it started ahead again.

The stallion jerked its head up at the stifling, stinking coal smoke. Lonergan patted the horse's wide neck and rubbed at the corded muscles and the skin. 'Easy, boy. Easy.'

Edward Lowney pushed open the screen door of his hotel lobby. 'Mr. Lonergan, you're not planning to be back in tonight?'

'No.'

'You'll be coming in, though. Remember this hotel, will you? And tell those Givren cowhands. Dobie is goin' to build a hotel section, but I thought my kind of place is what you'd want.'

'It is. I'll remember.'

'Then you positively will be back?'

Lonergan didn't raise his boot to the

43

stirrups. He watched the west end of Frontier, which was completely filled with the town's men, women, and children from the Drovers' porch to the bandstand. Kling and his five trail hands had come outside. All had liquor bottles in their fists and were yiping and giving weird yells and waving the whiskey at the saloon girls, who returned their calls and gestures from the second-story windows. The crowd opened a path and closed behind them. A gradual hush fell over the gathering as Herbert Rollins began to speak from the platform.

Lowney asked once more, 'You'll be in to ship your cattle, Mr. Lonergan? This is the town you'll use?'

'When I have stock to market. This is the closest town.' He walked the stallion and took his time moving around the left side of the crowd.

Rollins shouted his welcome to the cattle crew; his voice was unnaturally high and shrill to compete with the train engine's chug-chug and steam-wheezing, and the grating of the huge iron wheels backing along the steel rails onto the siding—that and the lowing and bawling noises made by the section of the herd that had been driven in alongside the platform. Coal smoke settled in a dense cloud above the area. It filtered out the brightness of

44

the sunshine and made the animals even more skittish. Three of the tall, heavy, long-horned steers had wandered out to the side of the crowd. Four additional older and wiser mossy horns had started to follow, pushing the first three nearer the people and bringing the close, heady smell of the cattle into the street.

Lonergan broke a path through to Loomis standing behind Kling and his trail hands.

'Sheriff, you'd better keep those cows back,' Lonergan warned. 'A hook of a horn and it'll be bad for someone.'

The lawman shot a glance past the two men who set up a tripod and photographer's camera out in front of the bandstand. The steers in so close grazed quietly on the bunch grass, their big tough-skinned heads moving up and down as if unaware of what the humans did.

'Hey, be sure them steers stay put,' Loomis called to a mounted cowhand. 'Watch the women and children.'

Rollins glared around and down from the platform at the sudden words. 'Loomis,' he demanded, 'hold it quiet so we can finish.'

'Yuh, hold it down,' one of Kling's crew echoed drunkenly. 'You keep quiet in this town, Sheriff. This is our town. Hear that?'

Rough laughter and talk drowned out anything the lawman could say. He shrugged

45

his shoulders at Lonergan, stood silent, and waited while Rollins motioned to the men at the camera. The black-suited members of the Town Council straightened and began to pose.

'Stop! No, stop!' a voice shouted. It was Kling. He'd thrown aside his bottle, sobered by a flick of a match in the photographer's hand. He tried to leap past the bandstand, but the crowd was pressed in so tight he couldn't get through. 'Don't!'

Lonergan was also moving, and Loomis near him, shoving men, pulling at them, throwing them out of the way as the photographer's chemical mixture exploded.

Children screamed, their eyes blinking, temporarily blinded by the burning flash. They grabbed for and pressed themselves against their horrified mothers or ran to their fathers. Their terrified cries and shouts mingled with the bawling uproar of the cattle.

Lonergan, his sixgun drawn, waved both arms at the nearest Longhorns. The cows, shocked at the flashing blast, had jerked up their heads, ready to run. The wildest, meanest steer lowered his horns and dug his hoofs into the turf.

'*Yaaah! Yaaah!*' Lonergan yelled, charging straight for the big heavy beast. Cattle close by, just as confused, paused in the same split second and waited for their leader to move.

46

'*Yaaah!* Back, *yaaah! Yaaah!*' Lonergan fired into the air over the steer's head.

The steer turned, and the close, heavy thud of his immense, solid hoofs was louder than the growing rush of hoofs beyond the tripod where the two mounted Texans kicked and spurred their horses to get clear of the beginning stampede. The steer, fully turned, horns tossing, started for the bend in the river, his animal instinct in complete control directing him toward the clear open flat.

For an instant, Lonergan could hear women's and children's screams and cries above the rising drum of the cattle. Then Kling was beside him. He grabbed his arm and whirled him around.

'Why'd you do that?' Kling demanded.

'They'd run right over the town. All these people.'

'They wouldn't! No! They wouldn't!' He cursed. Not drunken words, but hot hate-filled violent obscenities that bellowed above the earth-shaking roar of the hoofs. His fingers dug into Lonergan's flesh while both watched the thundering, crushing mass of cattle—four, five hundred animals now, with more joining as they neared the stock pens—charge wild and uncontrolled straight for the brush screening the Platte's muddy stream bed.

'You'll pay for this!' Kling threatened. 'Every head I lose, you make up! You hear! You'll make it up!'

Letting go of Lonergan's arm, he swung around to face Rollins. The cattle agent stood dumbfounded. He stared blankly at the cattle and the tripod and camera, which had been knocked over and crushed by the starting hoofs.

'Damned fool,' Kling bellowed. 'You damned fool! I'll kill you for this!' He started after Rollins.

Lonergan, a stride behind Kling, went after him; his left arm went up to grab and hold before the trail boss could draw and shoot.

CHAPTER FIVE

Lonergan caught Kling's shoulder. Kling, his palm on his Starr .45 butt, ducked aside to break the grasp. Lonergan gripped tighter and held.

'No! Don't!' Lonergan shouted. 'Don't touch him!'

Kling tried to complete his draw, but Lonergan threw his full weight against the trail boss' side. Knocked off balance, Kling went sprawling. He had to let go of the .45

and catch himself on the bandstand edge.

Rollins had backed to mid-platform. His mouth was wide open, his arms and hands extended, asking for understanding. 'I didn't mean it,' he pleaded. 'I wanted a picture for the papers. Of all of you, getting here with the first trail herd. That's all I wanted.'

'Damned fool,' Kling snarled. 'You damned, stupid fool.'

'I didn't mean that to happen. I didn't.' Rollins was close to breaking down.

Dave and Sid had moved in to back Kling. They watched the Colt in Lonergan's free hand. Their fingers were on their own sixguns; their faces were ready, all traces of liquor gone. More men crowded in behind them: town citizens, two tall men in cowhand's clothes—all just as confused and angry, and as willing to jump both Rollins and Lonergan.

'Hit him, Chet,' Dave said. 'I'll hold Lonergan.'

'I'll back that,' Sid said. 'Bust him.'

Lonergan loosened his grip on Kling's shoulder. The spectators who had hung on to watch scrambled over each other to get clear of the line of fire. The scuffing and the knocking of shoes and boots faded into a silence. The herd was a distant rumble, the only sound. Lonergan watched Dave and Sid

49

edge away from Kling to split the target. He kept his Colt pointed at the ground and made no motion to raise it.

'Don't make a mistake,' he said. 'Not for a few cows, Kling. You took the good time Rollins offered. Don't blame him.'

'He's bluffin',' a voice called behind Kling. 'He shot up one Texan today. Don't let him talk you out of it.'

'Don't, Kling,' Lonergan repeated. 'We'll help with your cattle. The townmen will give a hand.'

'I will, too,' Rollins offered. 'I'll help.'

Kling glanced at the cowering fat man on the bandstand. He spat at Rollins' shoes, but let his palm and outstretched fingers slide from the Starr's ivory handle.

'I'll see you later, you damned fool,' he said between his teeth. 'Dave, Sid, get after the herd. You men, give us a hand.' He took a step away from Lonergan, then slowed and gazed slit-eyed across his shoulder. 'We'll settle up later. You hold that check of yours. We'll damned well settle up.'

Lonergan waited. He didn't move his right hand until the pair on either side of Kling followed their boss toward the cowhands who were leading their horses from the Drovers' hitchrails. Rollins stepped down alongside Lonergan. The cattle agent was mopping his sweating forehead with his handkerchief. He smothered a sob as he watched Kling jump into the saddle.

'I didn't know,' he said. 'I wanted the pictures for advertising. They would have been sent to every paper clear to New Mexico and Arizona.'

'Those cattle had been driven almost a thousand miles. You knew that. A snap of a branch can spook a tired herd.'

'But I didn't know.' Rollins' jowls trembled as he shook his head. 'I'll lose my job. I got permission from my main office . . .'

'Mr. Rollins, you're lucky someone wasn't killed. You be thankful, with all those women and children that were here.' Lonergan left him and walked toward his big, black stallion.

Lowney had already gotten a horse and had ridden out. Halfway between the town and river bank, Ted Shane met the hotel owner, and the two of them headed after the stampede together. Kling and his crew moved at a gallop into the willows, the cottonwoods, and the thick brush that screened the deeper stretch of water. Lonergan had no way of knowing how many head would be lost. He did know that no dead steers were coming out of his own herd. He'd lived ten years for his cattle, had faced every troublemaker and gunfighter who'd tried to buck the law in his own town, and he'd lost the only woman he'd ever loved. He had come to Goodland for a full delivery of five hundred head. And he'd have every one of the five hundred when he pushed his herd west.

★   ★   ★

'They're all right, Chet,' Dave called. 'I can see our men. Chingo, Sanchez, McGuire and Lawson. None of them got caught in the crush.'

'I see. Swing in here. You town men, stay with him. You too, Sid.'

'Right, Chet.' He surveyed the man close to him and asked loudly, 'You, what's your name?'

'Bol. My pard's Lew.' Bol Jellison swung his bay mare in alongside Dave. He could see the four riders bouncing above the heads and horns of the steers that had gotten across to the far bank. Maybe seven, eight hundred stampeding south. The riders stayed at the edge of the run and crowded their horses against the leaders, jostling, driving them in closer and closer to make them turn. The main trouble was here along the river bottom. At least two hundred head had charged straight down the bank into the soft mushy sand, and they were bogged tight. Some at the

52

front that had been pushed and shoved and forced into the deeper water were gone—lost. They'd save the majority of the packed in, bawling and bellowing creatures that were smashing horn on horn while they hopelessly, helplessly tried to pull their hoofs free.

'Don't ride in there,' Kling shouted to a town man who had already shown he meant to get in very near with a rope. 'Two men to a steer. One down and one up. Watch it when they pull free.'

'You, Lew,' Dave waved, motioning wildly to the left. 'You two townies, handle this side with him. Bol, Sid, stay with me.'

Bol had halted the bay and was unhooking his lariat from the pommel. Quietly he told his brother, 'Lonergan's comin' down the bankin'.'

'Hey, Chingo's got them turned,' Chet Kling shouted to them above the noise and confusion of the stuck cattle. Far out on the flat, almost a mile's distance, the leaders had come about in a full circle and the stampede had begun to mill. 'They'll be headin' back to help.'

'We'll handle the ones this side the sandbar,' Dave answered. 'We won't need Chingo.'

Bol angled his mount against the swirl of the muddy stream and edged the horse flush

53

against Dave's. 'Lonergan's workin' toward deep water. He gets dumped over, it can't be connected to Robby.'

Dave had his lariat free and was separating the coil and noose to throw. Lonergan faced away from them at the near end of the bend. Shane was on the ground, moving into the mucky water while Lonergan, standing straight in the stirrups, swung his rope to let go at a bogged steer. The manila sailed easily over the Longhorn and was tightened immediately to take a strain. Shane, wading thigh-deep, grabbed at the jerking horns to work the heavy animal loose.

'He'll drift this way,' Bol said. 'I'll do it.' He sat bent forward, ready to spur his bay.

'Chet's too close,' Dave said. 'Lowney could look this way.'

Bol cursed. 'I wouldn't let Lew hit him. He's right where it can't be tied to Rob.'

'Wait. He'll be workin' 'til dark getting his own stock trailed.'

'Dammit, Dave. I held Rob up. I forced him to try alone. Now we got Kling against him, too.'

'Not 'til he has his cows. I want that herd.' Then he shouted loudly to a group of six town men who'd gotten ropes and had ridden to the water's edge. 'Three of you down and three up.' He pointed to where the muck hardened into gray sandbar. Some of the cattle struggled to shore alone. Others needed a little help and a man on foot could handle them. 'Careful, they might try to hook you soon as they're free. Watch them horns.'

'Yeah, we will,' a man answered. 'There's more comin' out to help. We want to help.'

Dave didn't answer. He'd picked out his first Longhorn and put his noose over the thick neck.

Bol also had his first steer. He'd made one mistake—had almost lost his son. He couldn't afford to make another, and he needed Dave and his other brothers to help get Rob home. A town man had the long horns and was trying to turn the bogged-down brute so his jerks at the head and the push of the current could take hold. Bol swung the bay more to the left and kept the strain on the line. The steer's hoofs, out of sight in the mud, came up inches, then suddenly sucked free. The animal plunged through the shallow water onto the firmer footing of the sandbar.

'Watch the horns,' Bol called. 'Work more from the side on the next one.' He coiled the rawhide and picked his second Longhorn.

*　　*　　*

Matt Lonergan coiled his muddy, wet lariat.

55

He backed his stallion onto the higher, solid length of sandbar. 'Two more left,' he called to Ted Shane, who was knee-deep in the water. 'I'll take the big steer next. Then the last cow. Careful with him.'

He raised the noose above his head readied for the throw. Ted Shane looked behind Lonergan and shouted, 'Hold it, Kling is comin'!'

Kling and the square-faced cattlehand named Dave splashed through the mucky black water. The pair, along with three more of Kling's crew and eight town men, had worked these last two-and-a-half hours a hundred yards below Lonergan and Shane. Yet not one word had passed between them. They were first-class cowmen, the way they'd done their share of the hard dangerous dirty work. Kling had seemed to be everywhere, shouting orders and directions, warning the men not to be careless, showing how to handle the bigger, uglier brutes that came out of the mud charging at the horses and the men who strained and pulled and sweated to free them.

Kling's clothes were as grimy and soaked and muck-splattered as Lonergan's. He'd lost his hat and now, bare-headed, his bushy black hair drenched with sweat across his forehead and down along both ears, he motioned at Lonergan.

'You want to sign them papers,' he called. 'I'm goin' up.' He turned his steeldust onto the banking. 'I counted eighteen head gone, Lonergan. You take the loss, or I don't sign.'

'Nineteen,' Dave added. 'Lowney and that sodbuster lost their last cow.'

'Nineteen, Lonergan. You're willin' to sign on that, come in.'

Lonergan stared across the eighth-mile of sandbar and the swirling river bottom to the carcasses that showed above the deeper water. He'd been as aware of the loss count as Kling. He was also as aware of the mass of black clouds on the northwest horizon, and that the air had cooled during the past half hour. Kling had picked his own time to make him decide. Either he and Shane and the other Givren riders gather his Longhorns before dusk, or they'd be stuck right here until tomorrow. Lonergan scanned the western horizon and shifted his gaze to the two beeves still bogged down toward midstream.

'Shane,' he said. 'Finish here and gather our tally on the north bank. I want the whole count.'

Chet Kling called, 'You heard what I said, Lonergan. I'm not takin' the loss.'

'We'll talk this over at the agent's,' Lonergan said. And to Shane, 'Get as many twos and long threes as you can. Not over fifty yearlings.'

'Right, Mr. Lonergan.' Shane waded deeper into the water and glanced at Lowney working below him. 'Get my horse. I'll stay in and you'll handle the rope.'

'Certainly.' The hotel owner came toward Lonergan, starting his stallion up the incline. 'Al Park'll get more hot water if you need, Mr. Lonergan. There won't be any charge for it.'

Lonergan nodded and jiggled the reins and let his tired horse keep his own head in making the climb behind Kling and Dave. A brisk, damp wind blew down, carrying with it the smell of rain and the pungent odor of washed sage. Jagged electric flashes cut through the black clouds. But the storm was still an hour off, possibly two, so distant that there was no sound of thunder.

Lonergan stayed directly behind Kling and the cattlehand until they passed the Drovers. The blonde in the yellow dress, who had been with the trail boss inside the saloon, waved from a second floor window. Kling didn't give her any attention. He dismounted at the land and cattle office and went onto the porch with Dave. James Hollis met them at the door. He held the contract in his right hand and pushed the screen door out with the left to allow Lonergan to step inside.

'Mr. Kling told you what he wants to do

58

about the lost cattle,' he began.

'What we will do,' Kling corrected. 'Either that, or no deal.'

Janet Duncan had stiffened behind her desk, listening to Kling's tone of voice. She watched the trail boss and Dave, and waited for Lonergan to answer.

Lonergan said, 'Read the agreement, Kling. Five hundred head of cattle delivered at the stock pens.' He pulled the bank check from his pocket. 'Twenty dollars a head. Ten thousand. It's signed over to you.'

'No you don't. I'll be damned if I take the loss. I've got a job to hold.'

'Mr. Kling.' Herbert Rollins' voice was loud and friendly, coming past the screen door. James Hollis had laid the cattle contract on his sister's desk. Kling glanced angrily at Rollins, but the heavyset man kept smiling.

'I waited for you to get back,' Rollins went on. 'I was told you lost nineteen steers and I wired Omaha. My superiors authorized me to subtract the cost of them from the shipping bill.'

Kling stared at him for another long moment. Without a word, he leaned over the desk top, took the pen, and made a hasty signature. He edged aside to let Lonergan sign. While Lonergan wrote, Kling said to Hollis, 'My boss will make other drives like this one. The price's twenty-five a head, delivered at the pens. We lost three, four days cuttin' off the Llano for Lonergan's gather. It either pays more, or we'll deliver at Dodge.'

'Well, I don't know,' Hollis started. He watched Lonergan.

Lonergan handed Kling the check. 'Twenty's all I pay. You deliver at Dodge, I'll pick any I order up myself and save the extra five.' He nodded to Janet Duncan and her brother. 'Thank you. I'll order by letter if I need more.' He walked to the door.

Rollins said, 'The cattle will come to Goodland. It will. Our company will straighten out costs.' He saw Lonergan's nod before the big man went outside. He looked toward Kling. 'I'm really sorry. I really am.'

'Keep clear of me, you damned fool. Just you stay shut.' The trail boss elbowed Rollins aside and moved past him to the door. Glancing around, letting Dave go by him, he added to Hollis, 'I'll cash this and pay your cut.'

Flustered, his jowls reddening, Herbert Rollins turned to James Hollis. 'I didn't want that. I tried.' He raised his right hand and slid it inside the breast pocket of his coat. 'I wanted to show him.'

Then, hurriedly, he walked through the open doorway.

Lonergan was just mounting his black stallion beyond the water trough and the hitchrails. Kling and his cowhand walked their horses behind him, headed for the saloon.

'Kling,' Rollins called. 'Wait, Kling.' He began to draw his hand from his breast pocket as he stepped hurriedly off the boardwalk into the street.

Kling stubbornly refused to look around. It was Dave who went into motion.

'Watch it! Down, watch it!' the cattlehand shouted. He shoved out hard with his left hand, knocking Kling flat. In the same moment, he went into a crouch, drawing his sixgun as he spun on his bootheels. He fired from the hip, once, twice. Both bullets struck Rollins square in the chest. Then Rollins' knees buckled and he twisted awkwardly as he dropped to the ground.

Lonergan whirled in the saddle, his Colt whipped up and out, cocked and ready. Both Kling and Dave ran toward Herbert Rollins, who was sprawled on his left side in the dirt. Men and women had appeared in windows and doorways. Hollis and Janet Duncan were already coming out onto their porch. The stubby, round-faced sheriff dashed from his office a block away.

Kling stared around and watched Lonergan

61

dismount. 'Damn fool,' he said. 'Tried to throw down on me. Dave was too fast for him.' His head shook from side to side. 'If it hadn't been for Dave.'

Dave halted over the dead man, his gun aimed downward as if he still wasn't sure of Rollins. He stretched one long leg and pushed Rollins onto his back. The dead man's coatfront was open, the hand across the chest in full view.

Dave stiffened his hunched shoulders at the sight of the two widening red blotches close together near the heart, and the silver-wrapped Havana cigar Rollins had been drawing from his pocket.

'What?' Dave muttered. 'He was drawin'. I saw him.'

'He wanted to give Kling that cigar,' Lonergan said. He didn't holster his Colt; he did not take his eyes off the weapon in Dave's hand. Loomis, puffing from his run, came to a halt opposite Rollins' body. He glanced from the bloody shirt to the cigar in the lifeless fingers.

Dave backed away, his sixgun coming up. 'No, you don't understand. He looked like he was drawin'.'

The lawman's hand froze before he had a chance to touch his holster. Lonergan, his .44 leveled, said, 'Don't make it worse, mister.

Don't try.'

Dave's muzzle inched toward Lonergan. Kling stepped in between them. 'He thought Rollins was drawin' on me.'

'Take it,' Lonergan told the sheriff. And when Loomis still paused, he said again, 'Take his gun, Sheriff. A man is dead. That's the first thing.'

Loomis was in beside Dave now and had the sixgun by the barrel. Dave's lips bit together. The expression of shock was gone; it was replaced by deep-lined hate.

'I'll get you,' he said. 'If it's the last thing I do, I'll get you, Lonergan.'

CHAPTER SIX

Loomis said, 'Over to the jail. Keep ahead of me.'

'No, he don't,' Kling said. 'Rollins asked for that, comin' out yellin' so fast.'

'He shot him. He killed Rollins.' The lawman's eyes flicked to the town men who had crowded outside. They circled in, their faces serious and watchful.

Kling stepped in front of Loomis, threw glances around them, and spoke more to the listeners than the lawman. 'Rollins had his

hand inside his coat. I thought he was goin'
for a hideout gun. It could've been me who hit
him if I was that fast.' His tone rose, louder
and surer, so the newcomers joining at the
crowd could hear every word. 'You want my
crew to come in. They don't get paid here
unless we get a fair shake in this town.'

A heavy quiet fell, and in the quiet the
sound of shoes and boots shifting on sand, the
rub of clothing against clothing, even the
quick intake of a listener's breath was audible.
Kling raised his stare to Hollis and Janet
Duncan. 'They saw it. They know Rollins
followed me outside. Ask them.'

'Lonergan, you were out here,' Loomis
began.

'He didn't see it,' Kling snapped. 'He was
ridin' away from us. I'm not listenin' to a
damn thing he says.'

A female voice spoke up from the rear of the
men. 'I saw Rollins follow you outside,' the
blonde with the low-cut yellow dress shouted
loud and quick. 'I was on the porch across the
street. Chet and Dave were right behind
Lonergan when Rollins yelled. Rollins was
reaching into his coat.'

'Hear her, Ernie,' a man said. 'She saw it
all.'

'Yes, Loomis. The cowhand's not to blame.
Don't you hold him.'

64

Ernie Loomis hadn't moved. He still gripped Dave's revolver by the barrel, the butt of the weapon held flat against his leg. Hoofbeats pounded on the roadway; three horses were heading into Frontier fast from the direction of the river. The lawman looked at James Hollis. 'Did you see it?'

Hollis spoke slowly and carefully. 'Rollins wanted to give Kling a cigar. That trouble they had.'

'I didn't see any cigar,' Kling snapped. 'Neither did Dave and you're not holdin' him.' His eyes swept the crowd, shifted to the horsemen pulling their mounts in at the back edge of the gathering. Sid, Bol, and Lew. Two more riders, then a third and fourth headed in from far out beyond the stock pens. 'You're not lockin' up one man from my crew.'

Bol was swinging clear of the saddle. 'What is it?' He shoved the nearest town man out of his path. Lew and Sid pushed in alongside him.

Kling repeated what he'd said and ended with, 'I'm not lettin' Dave be railroaded for that damned fool askin' to be shot.'

'You're right,' Dobie said. The saloon owner had broken through the mob with the blonde saloon woman. 'Katie Morrow saw it. She'll be at an inquest. We'll back you, Kling.'

'That's how it should be handled,' a town man agreed. 'The judge'll come in to hear this. I'll send my kid after him.' He looked around as the murmur started to grow. 'Loomis, he don't have to be taken in.'

'You've got his gun, Ernie. He can't do anythin'.'

The lawman studied the crowd and visibly braced himself. 'I don't know.' He spoke directly to Hollis. 'Did you see him draw?'

Hollis' head shook. 'It was through the window. Rollins went outside and called to Mr. Kling. We didn't see Rollins make a move.'

Loomis' gaze traveled across the circle of faces and stopped directly at Lonergan. Their glances locked, and the sheriff broke the exchange by looking away. He lifted an unsteady hand to rub his chin.

'If the judge will come in from his ranch,' he said.

'Dave'll be here,' Kling told him. He drew out the check Lonergan had paid him for the cattle and held it out to the lawman. 'I'll put up bail right now. Look, I got a herd to load.' And, when Loomis continued to pause, 'You think he'll run out? That ten thousand belongs to my boss. I ain't losin' my job for that. I ain't losin' it because I don't get the cattle loaded either. You hold the money,

Sheriff.'

'That's fair enough.' Dobie rubbed his hands along the garters of his shirt to keep warm in the damp wind. 'Kate'll appear. I'll see to it.'

'Let him work his cows,' offered a town businessman dressed in a black broadcloth. 'I believe Mr. Kling. He'll bring his whole crew here after. There are plenty rooms in Lowney's for them all.'

'We'll put some up at the Drovers.' Dobie saw the other businessmen agreed with him by the nods of their heads. They were letting him be their spokesman. 'I've got enough rooms for the whole crew. Mr. Kling, come on over before you go out and I'll give you the keys.'

More male voices spoke agreement. Most of them were the storeowners of the town, and their talk grew louder.

Ernie Loomis nodded. 'You stay in town tonight,' he told Dave. 'So I know where you are.'

'He'll be in. We'll all be back.' Kling, his mouth held tight and hard, eyed Lonergan, before he turned Dave and Kate Morrow toward the saloon.

Loomis said to Hollis and his sister, 'I'll be after you in the morning.' He nodded to Lonergan. 'You might've seen more than them. You be there.'

'I'll appear. Sheriff, you wanted to know how to wear that badge.'

Loomis had motioned for four bystanders to help lift Rollins. He wouldn't look at Lonergan. 'I am wearing it. I've got a wife and three young ones I'm wearing it for.'

'Then you think of them instead of the merchants of your town.' He took a step to move around the men carrying Rollins.

'Mr. Lonergan,' Alfred Park's voice said behind him, 'I'll take your horse over for a rub. He can stand a cleanin'.'

Lonergan began to shake his head, but the clop-clopping of more horses approaching from the flat beyond the bandstand stopped him. He watched the batwings swing in behind Kling and his cowhands and the small group of town men who'd trailed them into the Drovers. 'You take him,' he said. 'I won't be long, but you keep him off the street until I'm ready to leave.'

★   ★   ★

James Hollis and his sister were going into their office. Lonergan quickened his step to catch up with them. Janet glanced around at the scuff of his boots.

'You have your papers, Mr. Lonergan.' She watched him gravely.

'Are you staying inside?'

'No,' Hollis answered. 'I thought we'd go home.' His gaze lifted to the sky. The bottom rim of the sun was buried by the black clouds where it rested on the horizon. Thunder made a distant rumble, but there were not many lightning flashes yet. 'We have Lonnie at a neighbor's, and we want him home before the rain hits.'

'Could you leave the boy with your neighbor? Until after tomorrow?'

Janet lifted her head defiantly and met his stare. 'Lonnie's my son. I want him home with us. Don't feel you have to look out for us.'

Lonergan nodded slowly. 'You're being looked out for, Mrs. Duncan.' Janet and her brother followed his stare across Frontier. Kling and his cowhands and the town businessmen couldn't be seen inside the saloon. Against the brightness thrown by the ceiling and the backbar lamps, the silhouette of a man was plain to them, watching them from behind the batwings. 'If you have chain locks on your doors, make sure they're hooked.'

Both brother and sister studied the lookout. Janet's steady blue eyes were bright and unafraid; but her poise and dignity were too clearly an effort. She'd hold this illusion of strength and calm as long as he stayed, Lonergan knew; yet he wasn't impressed. He'd worked too long as a lawman to be fooled by externals. James Hollis wasn't as good at covering his feelings.

'They won't make trouble,' he said. 'We told the truth. Everybody heard what we said.'

'That wasn't an inquest. You go ahead and lock the office. I'll stay here until after you reach your home.'

Hollis shook his head, still not agreeing, or not wanting to agree. 'We told what we saw. Kling isn't foolish enough to try anything.'

'A man was killed right in front of you. Both of you. They're not fools, Mr. Hollis.' He gave a slight gesture at the cattle office. 'You lock up. I'll wait.'

Hollis opened the screen door, reached in, and slammed the inside door shut. He paused to stare beyond the Drovers toward the four horsemen entering town past the bandstand. The three at the lead were bunched together in the middle of the street. The last rider kept directly behind them, pushing his mount as hard; their faces were undistinguishable in the twilight. Biting his lower lip worriedly, Hollis pulled a key from his pocket and inserted it into the lock.

Janet Duncan asked, 'Are your men coming

in for a night on the town? That's what the newspaper write-ups promised. A wide-open cattle town.'

'Only one is my man.'

The watcher behind the batwings waved and called to the lead riders. The last man was Ted Shane, who slowed his buckskin once the others swung into the Drovers' hitchrails. Lonergan nodded at the saloon. 'Look, Mrs. Duncan. I've known men like Kling and his cowhand. That check wasn't handed over to the sheriff because they're afraid they'll lose out tomorrow.'

'That's right. They won't lose one thing in this town. You won't either. You cattlemen have what you want. You can do what you want.'

'I have what I came for. After the inquest I don't ask a thing from Goodland. I just don't want anything happening to you or your boy.'

'When every trail hand is gone,' she said. Her brother had both doors locked and was ready to leave. Janet hadn't lost her poise or defiance, but even in the thinning light he saw the corners of her mouth tremble. She tried to mask that with a weak smile. 'You answered the newspaper ads. We'd arrange for cattle shipments. The use of the stock pens is free. Goodland is a town where cowmen fresh in from a trail drive can tear loose without any worry.'

James Hollis took his sister's arm. 'That's enough, Janet. He's trying to help us. He's right about leaving Lonnie with the Stewarts. You don't have to keep that up.'

'If more of us had kept up the fight against the stock pens, Herbert Rollins wouldn't have been killed.' She'd spoken quickly, and a touch of color had come into her cheeks. She watched Ted Shane pull in his horse to dismount behind Lonergan. 'I wanted . . .'

'You wanted a better town,' Lonergan said. 'Now what you should want is the safety of your boy and your safety. You do what I want.'

The color heightened in her cheeks, but she did not give an answer.

'Janet, it'll rain,' her brother said. He nodded apologetically at Lonergan. Janet turned with him, and they headed toward the line of large, fine, white-painted homes with big glass doors on the north side of Goodland.

Lonergan moved to the center of the street and made it completely clear to the man watching across the batwings why he'd stayed close to Hollis and the woman. There was no way to be sure why Kling had left the lookout, whether it was for them or himself. He only knew he'd been through this before, so many times. The one certainty was that you never

72

actually were positive what to expect.

Ted Shane halted beside him. 'Cox and Rourke are waitin' the other side of the pens,' he said. 'People told us Rollins was shot. I'd've been in faster, but we were pushin' the cattle along the north bank.'

Hollis and Janet Duncan turned in at the fifth house. Lonergan's eyes flicked to the saloon. The lookout was in his place; he hadn't moved. He made no effort, and didn't seem to care if Lonergan or anyone else saw and understood exactly what he was doing.

'How many head do we have across?'

'Two hundred. Two-fifty, by now.'

'Good. That's enough for tonight. Get out and hold them, Ted. I'll be right with you.'

Shane took long strides to his horse. He glanced along the full length of Frontier while he mounted. Westward, the flashes of lightning threw yellow, bluish-red, jagged forks against the black cloud. Short bolts of chain lightning cut the thicker, uglier darkness to the northwest. The double rumble of thunder echoed along the curving river bed. Shane's expression had changed when he whirled his mount's stern and looked down at Lonergan.

'What's that one in the doorway got in mind?'

'Nothing for me. The sheriff's on to what

73

they might try.' He nodded at the lighted window of the jail. A shadow of a man, as clear and as watchful as the silhouette behind the swinging doors, studied the street. 'Take your time, Ted. Go ahead.'

Shane still didn't like it. He kneed his buckskin and walked the horse west.

Janet Duncan had gone into the house. Her brother hesitated long enough to strike a match and touch the flame to the wick of the porch lamp. Then, he followed inside.

The sheriff would check on them. He'd made that clear. Lonergan turned toward the hotel alleyway and saw that the darkening space between the buildings was safe for him to go through. He saw Loomis' body bend forward in the window to watch him. But he didn't see the man who'd been keeping lookout duck back fast into the saloon the instant he stepped across the thick heavy planks of the walk to cut down behind the Goodland Hotel.

CHAPTER SEVEN

Sid Jellison made certain he knew where Lonergan was heading before he turned and moved toward the drinkers along the bar. Bol and Lew met him between the tables. Sid muttered a curse. 'He's stayin', damn him. He's not drivin' that herd tonight.'

'His foreman went out,' Bol said. 'The cows'll hold.'

Sid's nod was quick and positive. 'Too damn long. There'll be more people than this town's ever seen in for an inquest. Could be too many headin' out with Lonergan if he waits 'til tomorrow.'

'He's gonna be pushed to leave,' Lew told him. 'Dave's settin' it up with Kling.'

Sid stared through the smoke haze to the far end of the bar. Kling and Dave had taken over the whole section of mahogany and brass, with a few of the town businessmen circled around them. The talk at this end concerned the shooting and how everyone felt. Sid didn't miss that, no more than he missed the fact that three of the crew were busy with the girls. McGuire and Lane had gone upstairs with big Chingo Hobb after the three had ridden in to find out what the gunfire was all about. Sid had known they'd come hell-bent-for-leather. If Kling needed one single thing, or if something happened to him, every last puncher was there to help or back him, or do his wanting exactly like Katie Morrow waiting near the bar end for Kling to decide when and how.

'That storm hits, it's too late,' Sid said. 'I think Dave . . .'

'Dave knows what he's doin',' Bol told him. 'He's worked in so's Kling has to back him. He's talked me and Lew in on it. When we do finish Lonergan, there's no chance it'll be tied to Rob.'

Again Sid nodded, just as sure and positive. 'That's it. The kid's so bad over there, the sooner we hit Lonergan the quicker we can get to talk with Rob.'

Dave saw them move past mid-bar. He raised a hand and beckoned to the bartender. 'Three more here, Dobie. Another glass, too.'

'Comin' right up.' The bartender pulled a cork out of a fresh whiskey bottle and hurried down opposite Dave and Kling. Kling pushed his shot glass out and fingered through his rumpled shirt pocket for the makings.

'Hey, Dexter,' the bartender called to one of the town men, who were gathered into a group of their own opposite the gilded backbar mirror. 'Give Mr. Kling one of yours.'

'Sure thing. Sure I will.' He was one of the best dressed, was long-faced, and had a wide bulge of stomach rounding out his gray broadcloth. He'd drawn a shiny silver case from his inner breast pocket. His companions and Sid and Lew crowded around when he

76

opened it. Six rolled cigarettes were offered. Kling laughed loudly. 'Wal, I heard about these, but never saw one.'

'Art got it from Chicago,' a second town man said. 'Straight from a jewelry store.' He was in his sixties, shorter than Dexter, his face veined and tight-to-the-bone. He grinned up and about him, his eyes good-natured under thick black brows. 'His wife and kids lick them up for him.' He added into the outbreak of guffaws. 'That's what I call really havin' it. Yessir, Artie's really got it.'

'Oh, no I haven't,' Arthur Dexter laughed. 'I bet you can see my Hannah rollin' these.'

Kling took a cigarette and placed it between his lips. A third town merchant struck a sulphur match and gave him a light.

Dexter said to Dave and Sid, 'Try them. Go ahead. I've been thinking of having some made to sell in my general store.'

'Good idea,' Dave said, taking his cigarette and meeting his brothers' glances as they accepted theirs. On the second floor, huge Chingo Hobb had appeared from one of the rooms with his saloon girl. Only Pratt to wait for now. Dave nodded for Sid to be patient— and to Lew and Bol. He didn't listen to the spiel the storekeeper went into about his business. He'd already caught enough of the conversation centred on Kling to know who

77

ran the haberdashery, gun shop, the pharmacy and the bank, and that Fullerton, the scrawny little boss of the livery, wanted first choice on the remuda they'd brought from Texas. Chingo was at the bottom of the stairs, and the woman with him holding his arm as if she couldn't let him go.

'Chet,' said Dave quietly. 'Pratt's all through.'

Kling lifted his shot glass and saluted. 'You got a good town. You people sure know how to make a man feel at home.'

'You just come in later,' Artie Dexter said. 'We'll hold the stores open 'til you finish loadin'.'

'We don't care how long you take,' added Charles Fullerton. A murmur of agreement traveled down the bar. It silenced when Kling nodded. The trail boss let the quiet drag out. A clap of thunder, close to the town now, rattled the windows.

'We've got a herd to load,' Kling said. 'We'll have enough to do holdin' the steers in the storm. Dave'll be back for the night, but he'll have to ride out early to help loadin' 'fore the inquest.'

'Mr. Kling, we weren't part of that,' Dexter said. 'Rollins and the cattle company handled everything.'

'Yeah, we didn't know he was crazy enough

78

to try takin' them pictures.'

'No jury'd do one thing to your cowhand. He had a reason for shootin'. We understand.'

'I reckon the inquest'll have to decide on that.' Kling waited and noticed that Dave also judged the temper of the town men and knew as well as himself they could get away with whatever they wanted. 'I'll have my crew in after the last train leaves tomorrow.' He gave Dexter a friendly pat on the shoulder. 'You get some of those ready-mades into your store, I figure you'll be sellin' them.' He nodded to Kate Morrow, who was leaning forward in her chair to get to her feet. 'We'll be in, don't you forget.'

'Remember, the town's all open for you,' Dexter said. Dobie's knowing grin included the women. 'We'll be waitin'. Maybe you can stretch it out two days, three.'

Kling slowed once he reached the swinging doors and let Dave and Sid push through with him.

'Hollis' house is fifth on the left, Chet,' Sid said quickly. 'No chance to get in the front. Law's in the jail window. Lonergan went down the hotel alley to check on his horse.'

'Okay, you'll take him with McGuire, Chingo, and Pratt. Cut him. Tell him he keeps goin' with his cows and he don't come back for any inquest.'

'I'll go, too,' Dave said. 'I want a crack at him.'

'You head out to the pens, so you can't be tied in. We'll shut them up. All of them. Move and let that sheriff see we're leavin'.'

'Listen, Chet.'

'No, you have to be clear. Put three of our crew with Givren's men and have them ready when Lonergan gets back.' He had his steeldust untied and turned the horse to pull himself into the saddle. A fine rain was in the air, actually more of a mist, but it was enough to make the walks and stirrups and saddle slippery. Another quarter hour, a half hour at the most, and the storm would hit. He let his mount swing its stern, heels chopping as the animal pivoted to pull away from the other horses and riders.

Dave rode abreast of him, then Sid. Bol, Lew, Chingo Hobb, and the others edged their mounts in close to hear. 'We'll keep ridin' another hundred, two-hundred yards 'fore you drop off,' said Kling. He held down his words and studied the darkened land while a roll of thunder echoed against the false-fronted buildings and into the alleyways. 'Bol, Lew, we'll go past the pens and circle north back to Hollis.'

No one spoke. The clopping of the horses' hoofs along the hardpack was as loud as the

80

grumble of thunder.

Passing the bandstand, Kling spoke out of the corner of his mouth to Sid. He nodded at the line of homes along the intersections of the cross streets. Everything was shut tight against the storm; no one was on the porches; no thin shafts of light were showing where a busybody might be peeking out to watch them leave.

'Move quick,' he said. 'Don't be afraid to make noise. Corner Lonergan and make him holler so anyone who's out will hear him and not the rest of us.'

'You'll hear.' Sid touched his long leather boot and pulled the top edge of a knife handle into view. Then he smiled at his brothers. 'You know how I do it. I promise, you'll be able to hear.'

*   *   *

A great clap of thunder shook the high double doors of the hotel barn, and small pieces of hay sifted down from the loft. The long, drawn-out shrillness of a train whistle came clearly through the damp, drizzly air. Lonergan, watching his black stallion finish the last of its oats, dug into his pocket and drew out two dollars to hand to Alfred Park.

'Oh, no,' the hotel handyman said. 'Mr.

Lowney is givin' everything for nothin'. Except the rooms and stall fees. He didn't eat that much.' He patted the horse's long, smooth neck. 'Certainly is a fine animal, Mr. Lonergan. You take mighty good care of him.'

'Keep this for yourself, then.' Lonergan slipped the bills into the red-headed man's side pocket. Another closer blast of thunder shook the rafters. The hotel surrey team, a set of matched gray mares, kicked at the sides of their stalls. The train whistle sounded again, nearer to the center of Goodland. Kling's crew had done a quick job of loading the first of the large herd and getting them tallied aboard the cattle cars before the storm struck with full force. Ted Shane and the others would have his own Longhorns where they could be bedded and held, even if the thunder and lightning spooked the calves and the yearlings. Lonergan stepped around the stallion to where Alfred had draped his saddle over the two-by-four between stalls. Reaching up, he pulled it down. He hefted its weight and walked with his slight limp to the horse's side.

'I've got it. Let me,' Alfred Park said. He turned to face the creaks of the opening barn door. Lonergan looked across his shoulder.

The door was pulled out wide. The three men who stood silhouetted against the glare of the lamp above the hotel's rear entrance were joined by a fourth. The last man, one of the group that had ridden in ahead of Ted Shane, led four horses. He trailed the others inside, out of the thick drizzle. A close flash of lightning illuminated the yard. The leader's bony, mustached face was smiling. He halted at the thick solid planking of the doorframe.

'Wal, I'll be damned,' he said; his smile was tighter, malicious, a drunken slur to his words. 'Lookee who's here. He's the one who made that sheriff take Dave's gun.'

Alfred Park edged close to Lonergan and gripped the heavy saddle. 'I'll put it on,' he said. And in a quieter voice he murmured, 'Watch out. They're all drunk.'

'You,' Sid said to Alfred. Backed by the bigger, huskier cowhand alongside him, he stepped toward the stallion. 'Forget that horse. I want my mount grained and rubbed.'

'Mine, too,' the huge man said.

'Mine after Chingo's.' The man holding the horses nodded to the fourth to shut the door.

Alfred Park saw that. 'I'm 'bout through. Just a second.' Watching worriedly, grunting, he threw the saddle over the black's spine.

'You'll do mine now,' Sid said. He paused while the door came in and slammed. The horses were left of the ladder leading to the mow, and his three companions spread out

83

left and right. Sid gestured at Lonergan. 'I want this stall for my horse. You put your saddle on in the rain.'

'Look,' offered Alfred Park. 'I'll handle every one of yours. Let me finish.'

'You dummy up.' Sid halted four feet from Lonergan. 'Move, or do I make you move?'

Lonergan nodded to Alfred. 'I'll finish with him. Handle theirs.'

'Out,' Sid snapped at Lonergan. He'd shifted his stance, and set his long muscular frame on the soles of his boots, continuing to bait Lonergan for Alfred's benefit. Lonergan knew they had no intention of letting him as much as leave the barn. He kept his side to Sid and watched the others from the corner of his eye while he tightened the cinch. He took the bridle in his left hand and began to lead out the stallion.

'Take them cattle and head west,' Sid said. 'You don't come back for anythin'.' He moved as if to allow room for Lonergan and the black. But when Lonergan's head was far enough past to stop a full view, he brought his right fist up in a vicious hook.

Lonergan expected something like that. Jerking aside, he let the bridle drop. He kept moving to the left clear of the horse and away from Sid. Chingo shifted his stance, blocked the barn's rear door. Both huge arms rose; his hands spread wide to keep Lonergan in the center.

Lonergan shot out with a backhand, caught Chingo in the pit of the stomach, and drove him into Sid's path. Sid, charging in, grabbed Chingo and hurled him out of the way.

'Close in, dammit,' Sid bellowed. Lonergan hadn't slowed and still moved nearer the door. Pratt, to the right, closed in patiently. McGuire circled around behind him, both arms outstretched to catch and hold Lonergan.

Alfred had the stallion in the stall. Lonergan felt a twitch along the left thigh. The hours of freeing bogged steers had tired the leg. The beating he'd take from these four could shatter the bone. He kept low and edged nearer the front door. Sid snarled an obscenity, threw a wild uppercut.

The blow missed Lonergan's jaw but hit the top of his shoulder, spinning him in almost a complete turn. Lonergan caught himself, slammed Sid with a solid right above the ear, and knocked him sprawling into the black's stall.

Lonergan twisted away and backed toward a corner. Pratt and McGuire moved in. Chingo still gripped tight to his stomach with his left hand. His right, like the other two, reached out to grab and pin Lonergan.

'Move back! Every one of you, move back!'

Ted Shane, sixgun in hand, pulled the high front door shut behind him. Chingo had frozen where he stood, ready to lunge at Lonergan. The click of Shane's hammer cocking was a loud metallic snap. 'You'll die before you touch him.' The muzzle jerked to one side, then the other. 'I want them hands in sight.'

Sid had pushed himself clear of the stallion. Alfred Park crowded the animal into a corner. On his knees, Sid felt with one hand along his boot top. He rubbed the skin and hair behind his ear; his eyes were mean and hot. His stare switched from Lonergan to Shane.

'Go 'head,' said Shane. 'Without usin' that. Finish it.' He grimaced at Lonergan. 'I saw them turn off soon as they left town. I let the rest go by and came back for a look.'

Sid was standing. 'Go 'head,' Shane repeated. 'Finish your fun.'

Sid shook his head. 'Not with a gun on me.'

'Damn, Sid, get him,' Chingo snarled. He coughed; his left hand pressed tight against his stomach. His right stretched out, caught Sid's shoulder, and shoved him at Lonergan. 'Get him!'

Cursing, Sid swung wildly. He hooked a left that missed Lonergan's arm and tried for the jaw with an explosive roundhouse. It was

86

wide by almost a foot, and Lonergan was on him. Lonergan hit him with a jab that drove him into a crouch. Lonergan's next punch loosened a tooth and sent a spurt of blood down Sid's jaw.

Sid tried to hold on, threw punches wildly, desperately, and caught Lonergan along the nose and square in the chest. Lonergan stood toe-to-toe for half a minute, knowing he could have handled it from a distance; but he'd just have a repeat of their tactics if he didn't end it once and for all. He speared Sid with a tremendous right that rocked him on his heels and followed up with a left and a right to the head. Sid, groggy, took the blows flush on the throat. He spun around and went crashing to the dirt floor.

Chingo shuffled a step forward.

'Stay,' Shane ordered. 'Right there!'

Lonergan stood above Sid, who fought desperately to squeeze air into his lungs. He sucked enough down to stop his panic and then lay absolutely still, giving all his strength to the painful work of breathing.

Lonergan leaned over, reached low, and drew a long-bladed hunting knife from the top of Sid's right boot. McGuire and Pratt exhaled drawn breaths; they didn't know what to expect. Thunder rumbled; lightning crashed somewhere close out on the flat. Rain had started, soft pings on the slate barn roof at first, but getting harder. Sid lay and stared at Lonergan.

'You tell Dave and Kling to do their own dirty work.' Lonergan balanced the sharp-bladed weapon in his hand. 'Tell them.'

'Sid wanted you for himself,' Chingo said. 'That wasn't for Chet Kling.'

'Chet'd do his own fightin',' Pratt added. 'You'll see later. Right now he's got cattle out there. He's too busy for you.'

Thunder boomed. Rain was almost a steady throb on the slates. Lonergan nodded, slowly. 'Don't make another mistake by trying to use your guns,' he said. Sid didn't utter a word and made no move while Lonergan took the bridle from Alfred Park and motioned for the hotel handyman to precede him toward Shane.

Alfred threw a fearful glance at the cowhands. 'They know I saw. I'm not goin' to stay.'

'You have your job with Lowney.'

'Only these couple days. He hired me only 'til they leave.'

Ted Shane said, 'We can use a man on the drag.'

'Sure. That's good.' Alfred grinned widely, then his long, bony face clouded. 'I ain't got a horse. I don't even have a war bag. I only got a

88

few things in my room.'

'We'll have an extra horse,' said Lonergan. 'Get your things and come on.'

Happily, Alfred Park left the barn ahead of Lonergan and Shane. Once outside, Lonergan pushed the door in and closed it. Shane swung into the saddle alongside Lonergan. He crouched over the horn, partly to shelter himself from the rain, but more to keep a good watch on the barn.

'They don't want any gunplay, but they might try hittin' your cows.'

Lonergan nodded, but didn't answer. The hotel's rear door had swung in and Edward Lowney stood in the square of yellow lamplight thrown from the lobby.

'You're not taking Alfred,' he called to them. 'He's working for me.' His tone raised. 'He didn't see anything, Lonergan. Don't you try forcing him into anything.'

'He wasn't forced,' Shane began.

'And he's not going to be. I worked all afternoon helping with that cattle. I just want to be left alone to do my business, and I'm not letting you steal my help.'

The full fury of the storm hit then. A jagged bolt of lightning struck south along the Platte and shot a fiery jagged fork up through the night into the clouds. The smell of sulphur was strong in the air. Rain came down as if a giant bucket had been emptied on the town. It beat against the slate roof, the deluge forming a wall of sparkling, foamy white against the partially obscured lamplight of the hotel lobby that vanished at the slam of the door.

Lonergan swung the stallion away from the hotel and the barn. 'Get back fast,' he said to Shane. 'Two men could have a bad time holding the steers in this.'

CHAPTER EIGHT

'That's all right,' Dave said. 'Lonergan'll damnwell be slowed down now he knows someone's on him.'

'He'll be lookin' out more,' Sid answered. 'Shane's comin' in so quick did it. We didn't see him.'

'Should've left one of us outside.' Chingo Hobb huddled his big body under the canvas overhang of the chuck wagon. He stared through the rain toward the squelch-squelch and plop of horses' hoofs approaching in the mud. 'Next time they won't pull that.'

Sid muttered something inaudible to the rest. 'Forget it, Sid,' said Dave. He'd looked away from Sid's bruised face and stood to watch Kling and the riders, who'd gone to the

Hollis house. During the time Sid had been telling about Lonergan, the storm had moved southeast. A flash of lightning beyond the Platte threw vivid, twinkling flame, brightening the entire area. Two of the watch met Kling with their questions. The hands who'd stayed close to the protected campfire bunched around the talkers, paying no attention to the steady downpour or how the tired, drenched horses kept sidling out and blowing and hammering and making wet leather strain.

'Hollis won't do any talkin'!' Kling was saying. 'Bol worked him over enough that he'll think damn long 'fore he answers anythin'.' The trail boss picked out Dave in the flickering light. 'You don't have to worry. The inquest'll be dropped soon as it starts.'

'It wasn't so easy with Lonergan.'

'Nothin' was lost. He'll have damn little to say from what he saw.' Climbing down, Kling went ankle deep in the mud. For a long moment the only sound was the rain and the suck and pull of boots and hoofs as the riders led their mounts away on their bridles.

Bol swore. 'You should've had a lookout, Sid.'

'We were four to one. We didn't expect anythin'.'

'You should've. I think of Robby, how bad

91

he is.' His words fell off, and he ducked under the overhang. Wind-whipped rain splashed in the canvas and splattered against the wagon side. 'Lonergan is out of the town. We still got what I want.'

Dave and Sid were quiet; they watched Chet Kling. Only Chingo and McGuire had remained along with Lew. They were as silent, looking down at the dancing firelight. Kling studied Dave, then Sid's swollen jaw, and finally, Bol and Lew. 'I'm a trail boss. My job's not to get mixed into gunplay.'

Chingo shifted his immense body. 'Their family got reason, Chet.'

'I didn't ask when I thought Rollins was goin' after you,' Dave said. 'I'm not askin' now.'

'I am,' Sid cut in. 'We used the name Johnson because we thought Lonergan might try meetin' the drive and takin' his steers early. We did our job.'

Kling nodded.

'Then keep on with us. Dave's trouble gets over with, we'll take Bol's boy down home. Lonergan's out along the river, and he'll be stopped.'

Kling stood absolutely still; he studied them but seemed to be listening to the noise and the movement of the cattle, and the thunder that grumbled far off on the flat to the south. 'I'm responsible for bringin' the money payment down to Texas. And my crew.'

'Lonergan's cattle'll be rangin' free,' Bol said. 'They're worth enough.'

Chet Kling's head shook. Chingo spoke first. 'They'd be for whoever picked them up.' He nodded to McGuire, and McGuire returned the nod.

Bol hurried an answer. 'We can use help. Dave's got to be let off 'fore we ride.' His eyes met Dave's and Sid's and he waved them to keep quiet. 'The crew'll be stayin' in that town, Kling.'

'They were promised a night. But they ain't a match for Lonergan's gun.'

'They won't have to be.' Bol stared to the northwest and the dark and the wind and the rain that blotted out all sight or sound of Lonergan's herd. 'Lonergan has to get back into that town 'fore he can give any trouble. Only he isn't gettin' back. He won't be givin' anyone trouble.'

*   *   *

Matt Lonergan was concerned about what might happen.

Not to his herd. Shane had chosen a fine spot, high and on smooth ground free of hillocks, holes, and stones. Despite the storm,

93

the cattle, held in by the riders constantly making their turns, had remained bunched close until the thunder and lightning had passed. Once it had, he'd spread the word to let the animals move about until they gradually settled. A long, rangy steer that had been picked from the point of Kling's drive had taken over, and it had been the first to bed down. There had been the usual movement at midnight, when the tired herd, in the instinctive way of cattle, rose almost as one and straggled slightly before settling down on the other side. They were quiet now, but Lonergan still had the feeling.

He knew trail crews, how they stuck together against a common enemy, that if one had trouble they all stepped right in and backed their own. He knew what lay ahead for Goodland, too, after the pressure of the inquest was off their minds. The cowhands already had lost one night of the hoorawing they had planned on every mile of the drive from the Pecos. They'd be wide open once they had the go, and the people would realize what they'd put in for with their advertisements and promises. Lonergan swung his arms across his chest to keep warm inside his poncho. Shane was warming himself on the left side of the bed ground. He could see Shane's shadowy form sitting tall in the saddle, and he heard the low thump of his fists.

There was something else. Lonergan sensed it. Something.

He held the black still, squinted against the damp cold overcast, and listened to catch a hint of a rider coming at him from the stockyards. Lowing and the small snort of a horse on night herd, a voice; the noises were short, flat, and toneless, just bits of sound above the rush of the river. Dark blots of men moved in front of the campfires the trail crew had built when the lightning and thunder had vanished below the southeast horizon. Other than that, nothing.

The town hadn't left his thoughts, the foolish moves made by the Council in trying to build up a name as a cattle shipping center. Janet Duncan and her son. Hollis. Janet had wanted so much more for the boy. He'd wanted the same thing, actually, both he and Eleanor, saving and planning all the long, hard years.

A sudden scuffing on the sand and the grass made him tighten on the quirt end of his bridle. The Longhorn that had suddenly wakened pushed itself erect, a heavy surly brute he'd had to haze back into place two hours ago when they'd made the midnight shift. Lonergan swung his big stallion and dropped his hand to the stock of his Winchester. A small calf had been startled by the first animal, and the calf's low bawl became louder. Lonergan jerked the rifle and pumped the weapon. It could be an antelope, drinking along the stream bed, or a coyote, or a wolf after meat.

The horse had taken only two stiff-legged strides when a faint metallic click came. Lonergan didn't have time to spur; he could only crouch and fall, diving toward the earth.

The hard, sharp smashing of noise from the left was part of the shock of the bullet's impact across the top of his shoulder. The power of the blow slammed him viciously into the drenched ground and made him roll once, twice, a third time before he had both hands on the rifle.

Shane shouted an order, his voice loud; the confused noise of the startled, wakening cattle drowned out the last of his words.

'Hold them!' Lonergan yelled. 'Keep them here! Shane!'

A gun crashed twenty yards away, close to the river. The bullet whined over Lonergan's head and whacked into one of the running cows with the sound of a loud handslap. The animal screamed and went down kicking.

'I've got the herd!' Shane was calling. 'Cox, Rourke, get them on that side! Drive them

96

away from the water!'

Lonergan was moving, feeling the warm flow of blood on his shoulder but no pain yet. He had the gunman spotted from the flash of the barrel, but he didn't dare fire. He crawled, slid ahead in the mud, and held the rifle ready.

The next shot roared, the bullet zinging past his bad leg into the spot he'd just left. Lonergan balanced the Winchester, separated the one tiny pinpoint in the dark, and put the bullet in low.

The gunman's weapon blasted into the air and almost blotted out the shocked, shrill scream of the man. Lonergan crawled forward and hugged the sodden sand to escape the next slug.

None came. Behind him the cow still screamed. To Lonergan it was a thick, piercing bellow, clear and terrible above the kicking and sloshing of the herd as it moved away from him.

Complete quiet out in front of him; the dying grunts of the cow close by. Lonergan's hands were icy. He listened for a groan, the sound of a hammer being cocked, the thrash of boots over the sandbar or through water.

After another minute, Lonergan held the Winchester out at arm's length and fired into the air. He dropped back fast, rolled a complete turn to the right, then another, and waited.

'Lonergan!' Shane called behind him.

'Stay back. Stay away!'

He waited one more minute, then pushed up onto his right knee. The left thigh throbbed—and the shoulder. Gripping the shoulder tight lessened the throb and deadened the twitching pain.

'Lonergan.' Shane's voice was even with him, going toward the river. Lonergan stood and moved carefully, his finger on the trigger; he was steady despite his limp.

They reached the cluster of willows the attacker had used for cover. Blood couldn't be seen in the dark. The deep prints of heels and a smooth water-filled depression showed where a man had lain. The side of the banking was dug out where he'd gone down to cross the Platte.

'There'll be tracks across there,' Shane said. He took a step.

'No, don't. He'd be too far away. He could've had a horse waiting.'

'He'll come after you again. This way . . .'

'I don't want you to,' Lonergan said. He increased the pressure of his fingers, controlling the bleeding and the white-hot pain that slashed down along the muscle of his arm. 'Get the cattle settled, Ted. Right now I need to get this arm fixed. I want to be sure I can hold my herd.'

CHAPTER NINE

Matt Lonergan slowed his stallion when the rangy, long-horned steer he'd been hazing closed back into the herd. He welcomed a little time to rest and gently ran his hand across the round of his left shoulder. The wound hadn't been as deep as he'd first believed. It had missed the bone, and the bandage he'd put on had stopped the bleeding. Ten minutes of being off the black at sunup to hurry breakfast before they'd gotten the column started wasn't enough. He needed more food and rest to control the weak feeling that came and went as if the strength and drive was slowly draining out of him.

He glanced around at the stock pens and the town off in the distance, the buildings and waiting cattle cars on the twin rails, the timber screen along the Platte, and the land all gray and dull under the overcast that had hung on the whole night and still showed no sign of breaking. They'd worked three hours, calming the cattle after the gunfire, readying them, and getting them moving. Six old and tough and wise steers that had been threaded out had practically made the point by themselves, giving Lonergan and the Givren riders time to work either on the swing or the drag, pushing stragglers back in or toward the front wedge. The column had formed easily, had stretched out loose, and then tightened gradually, striking a steady walk even before they'd gone a quarter-mile.

Ted Shane swung his buckskin from the opposite flank to cut between the steers. He didn't break the plodding gait of the cattle as he angled through them.

'I think we should hold this far out,' the Givren foreman said. 'It'll be easy enough to turn them when they're ready to drink.'

Lonergan nodded. 'Make as much distance as you can. I don't know how long the inquest will last.'

The bony weather-burned face stared eastward. 'I could go back with you.'

'No, none of you go in. If I bring anyone else, it'll look like I expect trouble.'

'There are more than thirty of them.'

'Just push the cattle as far as you can. I'll reach you all right. I'll give my testimony and ride out by sundown.'

The eyes under the wide-turned-down brim swept the humped, darkish outlines of the buildings again, then rested on Lonergan's wounded shoulder. 'That long? I figured by noon.'

'I'll stay to see Hollis and his family. Don't come in after me. You stick with the herd.'

Both men looked at the other two riders on either side of the column. They scanned the rolling line of backs and rumps, and the jerky swing of the horns. 'This is what I want,' said Lonergan. 'I'm depending on you. The three of you.'

Ted Shane nodded but said nothing.

Lonergan turned his stallion and headed for Goodland. He didn't know what his testimony would accomplish, no more than he had known exactly who'd tried to bushwhack him. They hadn't talked about it too much this morning, partly because he'd started Cox and Rourke forming the herd. Mainly, he hadn't wanted the three cowmen buying his trouble. It could have been a member of the Kling crew waiting to settle for one of their own. Or a kin of the Jellison he'd put on the jail bunk. And Lonergan fully realized he couldn't be certain of the townspeople. Not for one minute.

He circled wide along the prairie and traveled a good mile north, well clear of the river's screening timber, intent on going in from above the railroad station and the squat stone roundhouse.

*   *   *

The train with its eighteen cattle cars had already backed onto the siding above the stock pens. Its dark, black stack sent a thin, hazy spiral of smoke toward the overcast, keeping up its steam until the loading was finished. Lonergan circled east until he struck a rutted ranch lane that cut into Cross Street past the new, more substantial homes of Goodland. The smell of cinders and smoke was strong along this northern edge. The wireless operator sat in the depot, working at his desk under the Seth Thomas clock. A deeply tanned Mexican section hand, hunched over with the weight of a sledge hammer, walked on the ties checking spikes. Lonergan pulled in the stallion behind the jail's back door. Sheriff Loomis, emptying a porcelain water basin near the outhouse, had followed the horse and rider with his eyes since they'd turned off the road.

Lonergan could see the slight reddish tinge of the water. 'How is he, Sheriff?'

'He won't be comin' after you. You can leave your mount here and go across. I'll see it's brought out front.'

He said no more, but simply walked sluggishly, in through to his office.

102

Inside the cell block, the doctor watched beside Rob Jellison. The thin old man looked grayer, worn out from the long night. Jellison was unconscious, his gaunt face as pasty white as the blanket that covered him. His breathing was so shallow it was almost impossible to discern.

'Any family who'd let him go hunting a gunfight is crazy,' the doctor said. 'Plain crazy.'

Lonergan was silent. He stared down at the bed, his jaw muscles tight. He felt no pride in doing this. He was very tired. Too much had gone wrong. This young man charging in after him, the cattle almost stampeding into the townspeople, what had happened to Rollins, and to himself. He'd wanted to be so sure it would be different for him in this new life, but he had a problem potentially more threatening and vicious than he'd ever faced as a lawman.

He breathed in deeply, regretfully. 'Doctor, how long?'

The doctor simply shook his head. 'The bleeding took so much time to check. We haven't learned how to handle these things yet. Someday.'

'This will get out,' Loomis said. 'We can't keep it in.'

Lonergan stared down once more at the chalky, bloodless face. He turned to leave.

Loomis followed him to the barred, cell-block door. 'If there were more with him, they've only been waitin' . . .'

'Out there, Sheriff,' Lonergan said, and he made a short motion toward the street. 'It won't happen in here. It'll be out in that street you're supposed to control.'

Loomis looked bothered and irritated. His expression was similar to the one he'd had when Rollins lay dead in the exact spot town citizens now crossed on their way to the courtroom. It was more pronounced today, less cautious. Yet, there was a lot of difference between caution and the way the lawman straddled the high fence. Lonergan moved outside and onto the boardwalk.

Loomis stopped close to the doorway and stood there staring through, rubbing his chin as he watched Lonergan. In the long silence, Doctor Kanter stood alongside the cell bunk.

'He's asked for what will come,' the doctor said in a serious voice. 'Won't help to watch him.'

Loomis merely nodded. 'He's out there alone. He knows that clear enough.'

'That's the only way it can be. He knows that, too.'

Suddenly Loomis swore. He smiled bitterly and said, 'You know what I want to do, Doc? What I know I can never do?'

Doctor Kanter nodded, thoughtfully. 'They'll all be gone in two, three days. There's talk of holding another vote at the town meeting.'

Loomis didn't answer. He sucked in a deep breath and concentrated on watching Lonergan and the west end of Frontier.

★　　★　　★

The stillness warned Lonergan. It wasn't a silence; there was the same hidden sound, like the hungry, low-pitched growlings of animals, persistent, grating to his nerves. People, mostly men, waited at the town hall porch for the courtroom to be opened. A few storekeepers hooked back their doors; railroaders and Irish and Mexican section workers headed toward the roundhouse; here and there an early shopper went into a building. How many times had he moved up the same dirt street, eyes watching him, waiting? How many times had the thin low-pitched sound been felt, sensed rather than heard? Like the singing tension of a wire drawn too tight.

Lonergan slowed his pace to allow a ranch family to pass in their buckboard. He studied the expression on the father's face and he could see he didn't even slightly resemble a

Jellison. He continued on, as if he hadn't noticed the questioning stares of the children, who were crowded into the wagon bed. In front of the hardware store, he simply nodded to the gangling youth who was wiping down the store's high, wide window. He didn't expect any sign of recognition, and got none.

He could see Janet Duncan and Hollis now, in the group on the courthouse steps. Neither the brother nor the sister looked his way. They watched, along with the rest of the citizens of Goodland, the lone rider who entered their town from the direction of the cattlepens.

Dave sat his saddle straight and easy, and looked neither to the right or left. He wore the same stained, work-faded trail clothes, his wide-brimmed sombrero pulled low over his eyes. Lonergan could not see his face plainly, just the tilted-down brim and the square jaw with its black growth of beard. Dave rode too calmly, too casually to be the one he'd hit last night, thought Lonergan. He didn't have on a gunbelt. Passing the last intersection, Lonergan caught the remarks that were made about Dave's being unarmed. And about his coming in wearing his Colt.

Hollis and Janet Duncan entered the courthouse with a short, elderly man in a dark suit, with a Lincoln beard and a tall, black hat. Dave headed straight for the hitch-rails. He gave no notice to Kate Morrow and the other saloon women standing on the Drovers' porch. He tied his dun horse and went onto the steps before Lonergan reached there. The cowhand acted as if he were alone and intended to face the inquest alone.

A momentary outbreak of talk sifted through the people along the walks. Then, almost instant quiet fell. The hush was somehow louder than gunfire. Lonergan paused and glanced westward.

Kling's trail crew came in slowly, almost sedately; every last horse of the twenty-six kept at a walk. The people who'd stayed inside the stores to do their shopping filed out of the doorways onto the porches and steps. Faces that had shown interest expressed something different now. Men's throats and jowls became tighter, their eyes more watchful; women backed to the rear of the porches.

The riders, every one of them wearing a sixgun, every saddle scabbard showing the stock of a carbine or rifle, filled Frontier from walk to walk. They didn't glance to either side: twenty-six dusty, thick-bearded men, breaking off, without a word, into groups of two, three, and four to ride to the tierails at the saloon, the town hall, the hotel, the jail, and even the cattle office.

They didn't wait around and smoke or talk like the town citizens. As they split up they re-formed into one large bunch and walked onto the courtroom steps. The group crowded the long porch, then went inside.

★　　　★　　　★

Lonergan studied Janet Duncan and her brother while the judge went through the technicalities of swearing in an inquest jury. It was plain that James Hollis wasn't himself. He hadn't as much as glanced around the huge courtroom since he'd sat down; he simply bent forward a bit, waiting, his body tense, his spine and shoulders taut. He either hadn't had any sleep or he was terribly worried about what might come. His sister's composure was faltering. Her posture wasn't as straight; she was overly attentive to her brother. She didn't shift her eyes from him, but stayed so close it seemed as if she was taking care of a small child.

The judge was an old man, past seventy-five. He shot sharp glances at the witnesses and spectators, brushed a hand through his beard and rubbed at the wrinkled skin of his forehead. The people buzzed with interest and expectation. Dressed in their Sunday clothes, the men and women crowded the rows of seats. They were in sharp contrast to the trail crew that had bulged through the doorway and spread out quick and deadly down both side walls and the rear of the room.

The jury was in place. The gravel rapped. 'Matthew Lonergan,' the judge began.

There was a noisy, rough shuffle and scraping of boots and chairs. Kate Morrow stood at her chair. 'Lonergan didn't see the shootin',' she called out loudly. 'His back was turned. I was on the Drovers' porch, and I was the only witness to the shootin'.'

A quick rapping by the judge stopped her; and the rough grumble among the cowhands and the chatter subsided. 'Sit down. You will be heard, Miss Morrow.'

'But Lonergan shouldn't even be in here. He didn't see anything. Only I . . .'

'You'll have your turn.' And to Lonergan, he said, 'You aren't being sworn.' He held up the Colt revolver Loomis had taken from Dave. 'This is the weapon you saw the sheriff impound after the killing?'

'Yes, it is.'

Low talk rumbled through the courtroom. Raps of the gavel silenced it. 'James Hollis,' the judge said. 'Will you come forward.'

Hollis got to his feet hesitantly. He made the slight pause appear that he used the time

109

to speak to his sister, but odd, deep lines were cut into the corners of his mouth. The lines stiffened while he straightened fully and took the first step toward the witness chair. He did not, or would not, meet Lonergan's eyes.

The fact that Hollis gave nothing as evidence wasn't a surprise to Lonergan. Hollis stared at the floor during the oath and the judge's opening question. When he answered, he glanced at his sister and stated that he couldn't see anything last night because of the porch lamp glare, ending with, 'I shouldn't be a witness, Judge Roddy. Neither should my sister. We didn't see a thing.'

'You told the sheriff that Rollins had raised his hand to his coat pocket.'

'Well ... he had his hand in his pocket before he left my office.'

'Did he say anything about a cigar? Did he say he was going to give Kling a cigar?'

Hollis was thoughtful, his eyes lifting for a fraction of a second to Kling and Dave, who were sitting on the front row. Outside, the muffled blast of a train whistle was followed by the low grinding and chuffing of the engine coming off the siding. Hollis said, 'I don't remember that he did. No, he didn't. He just went out after Mr. Kling. That's all we saw, either of us. When we ran onto the porch, Lonergan and Sheriff Loomis were closer to

Rollins and Mr. Kling than we were. And that's all we know.'

Lonergan leaned forward and watched the judge twist his bony fingers around the gavel. Dave sat quietly, his attention on the witness. Kling smirked and made a remark to Sid, who was beside him. The fight had been harder on Sid than Lonergan had realized. The right side of his nose and cheek were bruised and swollen, the bluish color making the skin and mustache dirtier and adding to the hard, hateful eyes and the tight-clamped mouth.

'All right,' the judge asked. 'Tell exactly what you saw of the actual shooting.'

Hollis inhaled, quickly exhaled. 'I told you. I didn't see the shooting. Neither did my sister.'

'Mrs. Duncan will answer for herself. You give your story.'

'Judge, I did give it. That's all I can say.'

'You were in your office. Lonergan left.' He watched Hollis' short nod and was aware he'd gotten him tense again. 'Rollins was in the office with Kling and Dave. Was there an argument or a fight?'

'No. Kling signed the cattle papers and they left.'

'He didn't have words with Rollins?'

'Judge, I told you . . .'

'Did they have words, Mr. Hollis? Answer

111

my question!'

Hollis' head shook. 'They didn't have an argument. Mr. Kling signed and shoved Rollins out of the way...' His mouth clamped shut and he was suddenly frozen to the chair, staring directly at Kling. The trail boss shifted his stance against the back wall and glared at Hollis. The whistle of a train far off in the distance punctured the sides of the room, sounding very loud and shrill in the dead silence.

Kate Morrow was on her feet. 'Judge,' she called. 'I was the only real witness.'

Chet Kling stepped close to the back line of chairs. 'Shut up!' he told the woman. 'Sit down and shut up!' The members of his crew near Sheriff Loomis in the rear doorway watched every movement the trail boss made, and they waited. Spectators squeaked in their seats, shuffled boots and shoes, coughed or muttered hasty, low spoken words in their effort to settle down.

Judge Roddy asked, 'What happened after Kling forced Rollins out of his way?'

'He didn't force him. Not really. Mr. Kling didn't like Rollins. I don't blame him after the stampede Rollins caused.' Hollis rubbed both his palms together. He looked very confused and frightened, and couldn't seem to take his eyes from Kling or Dave. 'Rollins wanted to talk, and Kling brushed past him. That's what it was. He and Dave brushed past him and went outside.'

'And Rollins followed him. He hadn't provoked Dave?'

'No. He just went after them to call to them.'

'Rollins called to them. Was it a loud call or a soft one?'

James Hollis shrank down in the chair. He would not look at the judge. 'It was a loud call. Loud enough for us to hear.'

'Did it sound like a challenge?'

Hollis didn't speak.

Judge Roddy said, 'Jim, I don't want to have to drag every word out of you. You were there. Tell what you heard when Herbert Rollins left your office. Every word.'

'It could've been a challenge,' Hollis admitted. 'If Mr. Kling thought it was, he had a right to draw. The Council voted to let cowhands wear guns in this town. If they wear them, they've a right to use them when they're threatened.' He glanced up, and his gaze shifted back and forth across the listeners' faces. 'That's right, isn't it? If a man is allowed to use a gun, to carry it, I mean. I mean he can use it?'

Judge Roddy said, 'Step down, Jim.' He rapped the gavel abruptly. But Hollis didn't move to leave.

'I've told you everything, Judge. My sister saw exactly what I did. She can't tell you any more. Take my testimony for both of us.'

'Step down,' the judge repeated. He rapped the gavel louder to calm the outbreak of conversation, then he turned toward the jury. 'It is clear there is much more to this shooting than the present list of witnesses can fully explain. This inquest is recessed until nine o'clock tomorrow morning.'

'What?' cried Chet Kling, straightening to face the bench over the tops of the heads. 'You can't recess.'

'Don't you tell me what I can't do. This is federal jurisdiction.' His wrinkled face above the Lincoln beard was as hard and determined as Kling's. 'David Johnson and you, Mr. Kling, will agree to stay in Goodland until that time, or I'll see both of you named as fugitives from justice. Don't you tell a court of this county and country what it can or cannot do.'

Kling glanced around at the sound of scraping chairs. Every member of his crew stood poised and ready. The townspeople cowered in their seats, caught between the judge and the cowhands.

'We have to start back,' Kling said.

'You'd planned to stay tonight,' said the judge. He eyed Lonergan, who was on his feet and edging closer to Hollis and Janet Duncan. Lonergan watched the trail crew, Kling and Dave particularly.

Then Judge Roddy stared at Dobie, Fullerton, Lowney, and two or three more owners of the town businesses. 'You were going to stay, Mr. Kling, and the stores and saloons are ready for you.' He leaned on both hands across the desk. 'This inquest will continue at nine o'clock tomorrow. The rest of your men may leave, but you two be here!' He rapped the gavel and motioned for the bailiff to open the doors.

Kling stood for a long, drawn-out second. He didn't look at the judge, or at Hollis or Janet Duncan, but only at Lonergan. Turning, he stalked out the front door. The trail crew didn't wait. Dave had left his chair. He brushed roughly past the men and women who'd started into the center aisle. At the door he joined the cattlehands who were moving as one ominous, silent body down the steps and into the street. Dobie and his saloon women, and three or four other town storeowners trailed in their wake.

Judge Roddy stepped around the witness chair to Hollis and Janet Duncan. 'You can go out to my ranch for the night,' he offered. 'It'll be bad enough with a trail crew in without another problem.'

'We'll go to our house,' Hollis told him. 'We'll stay in our own house.'

'Jim, I want to talk to you later. I'm going door-knocking and see if I can find someone who saw what went on out there. I need you and Janet at the inquest tomorrow. I don't want anything happening to you.'

'We'll stay inside,' Hollis agreed. He took his sister's arm.

Lonergan said, 'I'll walk down to your house with you.' Janet Duncan had kept her back to him, although she was fully aware that he'd stayed close behind them. 'No, not you,' she answered. 'That might not have happened if you weren't here. The first gunfight you were in. It made the second shooting so easy.'

'You'll need protection.'

'They'll have protection,' the judge said. 'I'll have Loomis swear in extra deputies. They'll watch the house. Lonergan, you stay, too. One of the deputies can ride out to your herd and tell them you'll be here a while.'

Lonergan nodded, and the judge walked ahead of them up the aisle between the rows of empty chairs.

Outside, the crowd had drifted from the porch and had strung out along the roadway. Kling and Dave weren't in sight, nor were the cattle crew. A tinny piano played 'Buffalo Gal' inside the Drovers. A second train that had

116

come in backed its empty cattle cars down the siding, its stack giving off huge blobs of black smoke that shifted and drifted toward the breaks in the overcast. Sunlight that slanted through the blue spaces splattered on the wet leaves of the cottonwoods and the aspens along the riffles and curves of the Platte. With more wind-blown cloud thinning, sun-glare shone dazzling white on the high sandbars jutting out into the stream.

Lonergan halted on the top step and watched the sheriff and Judge Roddy move past the intersection and go up Cross Street with Janet and Hollis. He waited until the four had reached the Hollis lawn. Then he stepped down into the roadway.

He'd seen the shadowy figures of men in the open jail doorway and believed they were the deputies Loomis would swear in. It was the doctor who appeared first, hurrying out to shout to someone. The tall, whiskered Bol, coming outside with him, grabbed the arm of the old man's black suit, shoved him out of his path, and cut off what he meant to do.

'Lonergan!' Bol Jellison yelled, blurting out the name, making it sound like something foul and crawling. 'He's dead, Lonergan! My boy's dead, and you killed him!'

Four men conversing in the middle of the street ducked aside and left the space between

Lonergan and Bol wide open. Bol half-ran off the walk, his right hand stretched loose and long, his fingertips touching the butt of his sixgun.

'Draw!' he snarled, coming closer, his voice louder and more vicious. 'You killed him, Lonergan! Draw!'

CHAPTER TEN

Boots and shoes kicked, raised the dust, and clomped on the walks. A woman shouted shrilly to her child, urging him to run for a porch. 'Get the sheriff,' a man called. 'He'll kill him,' another warned. 'He ain't givin' Lonergan a real chance.'

'Get Ern. Get the sheriff!'

'Ain't time! Out of the way! Back! Quick, move back!'

Lonergan's hands rested flat along his sides. Sweat dampened his palms and broke out across his shoulders and under his arms. 'This won't settle a thing,' he said, holding his body stiff. 'No more than it did for the boy.'

'It'll end it,' Bol whispered. 'Draw, or I'll drop you right like that.'

Loud, confused, fearful voices had yelled into the Drovers Bar and now the piano had stopped. The iron batwing hinges grated loudly, wildly, while men poured onto the porch. Kling's shout blasted the stillness.

'Stop it, Bol! What the hell . . .'

'This ain't your business! None of you! Keep out!' Bol's eyes had not changed focus, but stayed riveted on Lonergan. Bol's mouth twitched and spittle dribbled from the left corner down into his thick black beard. 'Make your play, Lonergan!'

Lonergan hadn't moved. The distance between them was less than fifty feet. Neither could miss, and with the edge Bol had, he'd have to use the first precious instant to duck away. People near both of them were a blur; only Bol was in his view. He heard shouts to his left coming from Cross. He heard, but didn't let his mind catch the words. Only Bol standing there was real. Lonergan inched his hands up, palms open, showing he didn't want to draw.

'This is foolish,' he said. 'A waste. No, Jellison.'

'Draw,' sneered Bol. His fingers jerked at the butt.

'Bol!' Kling yelled. 'No, it's murder, Bol! No!'

Lonergan leaped to the left and fell hard and fast away from Bol's gunhand. His fingers reached for his holster, his left leg outstretched, poised to hit the dirt and hold him erect while he fired. Bol's first bullet caught along his pantsleg. It tore into the cloth and sliced through the thick leather of the boot, knocking Lonergan down faster and throwing off his draw.

Lonergan struck the ground and rolled in the dust; as his shoulder hit solid earth and spurted blood, a slashing wave of agony coursed through his arm. Bol's second bullet whapped the dirt inches from his head. He stopped his roll and turned flat onto his spine, his Colt cocked. Bol's tall form towered against the sky, blocking out the buildings behind him. His bearded mouth was wide open, laughing; his weapon, held out for a finish shot.

Bol died happy, believing he'd killed Lonergan.

Lonergan's single shot caught him directly over his heart. Bol's body straightened, jerked back, driven onto its heels by the impact. His last bullet hit a yard from Lonergan's head and exploded in a bomb-burst of sand. He buckled forward, his sixgun still gripped tight, and dropped like a felled tree.

Lonergan pushed up onto one knee and aimed his Colt at Kling and the cattle crew, who were closing in on him.

'Stop there. One move! Any of you!'

Dave threw both arms straight out and stepped ahead of Kling. 'I ain't carryin'. I'm not, let me see him.'

'You got another try comin',' a voice snapped in a Texas drawl. 'Lonergan, you get up!'

'No! No!' Kling ordered. 'That's enough, Lonergan.' He whirled about to face his crew. 'Bol asked for that! Don't push it!'

'Dammit, Chet! He's got it comin'!' Chingo Hobb, standing huge and threatening, answered. 'What in hell you pullin'? You kept us outa town last night! You don't want us to drink in there! Now this!'

'Get back inside,' Kling ordered, his eyes on the leveled weapon in Lonergan's hand. 'Dave, Sid, take care of Bol.' Chingo kept moving forward, and Kling's fists doubled. 'Back, Chingo! I said back!'

The big, ape-built brute halted and glared at Lonergan. 'Bol was that dead kid's paw. He had his rights.' Six, then a seventh and an eighth man edged behind Chingo. Their weather-roughened faces were surly; their eyes, hard as they watched Kling and Lonergan. Then their stares switched to Dave as he bent over to check the dead man.

'You're goin' to try takin' him with that gun in his hand? Get over to the bar.' Kling nodded at Bol's body. Dave and Sid were gripping the arms and legs to lift him. 'Get over. All of you.'

A cowhand said, 'We don't like it, Chet.'

A second muttered a curse. 'We damnwell don't, Kling. We don't owe one thing to this town.'

Running boots clomped in the roadway. Sheriff Loomis, Judge Roddy, and two young townmen headed for them. Loomis and the two held sixguns up and ready. Kling's voice hadn't softened, but there was more of a warning than an order to it.

'Bol knew what he was tryin'. We get back into Dobie's. Now.'

Muttering and swearing rumbled through the tight-packed cattle crew. One, a second, then more at the rear turned. Kling spoke to them all, but his stare followed Dave and Sid as they struggled with the lifeless body. 'I'll buy the first drink. They promised a good time,' Kling said. 'I have to stay for the inquest, but we can enjoy the waitin'. We get the good time we were promised!'

'Damned right we do,' Dave said. His eyes bore into Lonergan's, then flicked to the dark stain of blood that drenched the left shoulder.

'You get that fixed,' he said. ''Fore this is through, you'll damnwell need both arms, Lonergan.'

122

Sheriff Loomis halted in front of Lonergan and looked from him to the dead body being carried toward the line of horses at the Drovers Bar hitchrails.

'I'll take that gun. Over to my office.'

'He didn't start that,' a man said. 'He woulda been killed.'

'Yeah. He tried to talk out of it. He did, Ernie.'

'Well, for his own good,' Loomis began.

Judge Roddy interrupted. 'Lonergan did try to keep out of a fight. Loretta and Paul Hoover heard it from the bank. The Murrays were with them.'

'He was in a gunfight,' Arthur Dexter said. The store owner had pushed to the front of the circle of faces around Lonergan. 'That's twice he's had shootouts since he's come, and I think . . .'

'You think?' Judge Roddy mimicked, keeping his voice just as tense and high-strung. 'You should have thought before you took part in the ridiculous idea to bribe the cattle drives with all sorts of promises.' He gazed at the saloon. The cowhands were filing in past the slatted swinging doors. Kling and Chingo Hobb and three men at the end had paused to watch the crowd. The judge's stare returned to Dexter and included the store owners and Lowney and the other town businessmen near them. 'You should have realized something like this might happen once you open up a town.'

Loomis said, 'Doc better look at that arm, Lonergan. You should get a place to stay tonight.'

'He doesn't use a room in my hotel,' Lowney told the lawmen. 'I don't want that kind of trouble.'

'And you've got no right offerin' him anythin',' Dexter put in. 'Loomis, you know what we think.'

Lonergan moved from the group. His shoulder was throbbing. He held onto the round of the bone and pressed the tender area. Judge Roddy trailed after him. 'My office is upstairs,' he offered. 'I'll have the doctor tend to your arm up there.'

Lonergan shook his head. 'I don't want people to have something to say after the inquest. I'm still a witness.'

'The doctor's house is the second on the right. Around the corner.'

'Thanks, Judge.' Fresh blood seeped through the cloth to his fingers. A new wave of heavy tiredness flushed down through his body. 'I'll see him.'

'Watch out for yourself.' The judge was

staring toward the Drovers. Dave and Sid had joined Kling at the batwings. Through the long half-frosted saloon window, faces watched Lonergan and the small knot of town businessmen who followed Loomis into the jail office.

'You have to find a place to rest and stay safe,' the judge said. 'I want to keep all the witnesses I can get for tomorrow.'

'Then have that sheriff keep a good watch on Hollis and his sister, Judge. I'll get fixed up. I'll be there.'

CHAPTER ELEVEN

'Is he coming here?' James Hollis asked. He had unlocked the kitchen door to go through the back yard. 'Janet, is Lonergan coming here?'

'No, he's going into the doctor's.' She let the starched lace curtain fall into place. 'We shouldn't do this. The deputy will be outside. Even if we told Lonergan.'

He twisted the key in the lock again. 'That would be the worst thing. I've had as much as I can take with one beating.' Unconsciously, he touched below his ribs on the left side. 'All they need is to see us talking to that man.' He

125

leaned over and grimaced while he lifted the heavy leather suitcase Janet had hastily filled with their clothes and Lonnie's. 'Watch. We've got to get going before Brad Gillis starts movin' around the house.'

'James, I'm not sure. Running never settled anything.'

'It'll keep us clear of that gang. Think of Lonnie. Once he comes home, he'd be the one they'd hurt to quiet you.'

Janet looked doubtful. 'It would only be until after the inquest.'

'Not if the judge holds them for trial. They couldn't protect us that long. You know the judge didn't want the stockyard. He'll force a trial.'

He snapped the key again, opened the door, and studied the quiet of the yard. 'I'll signal when I have the buggy hitched. Just go to Paparo's and get Lonnie and meet me.'

He stopped outside, closed the door quietly. They had a chance now, he knew. Once they were clear of town on their way to Omaha where they could get real protection, they had a good chance. That thought was the only thing that was clear in the mind of James Hollis.

★　　★　　★

'Hollis, damn him,' Dave said. 'He's got to be shut once and for all.' He'd gone directly to the saloon's rear door and paused only long enough to check that Dobie and his women were so busy they wouldn't see him leave.

'Crazy,' Kling told him. 'You can't try to use a gun.'

'I don't need a gun, not for him. Bol started it last night, I'll make sure he clams up tomorrow.' He cut his words short until three cowhands and their girls went past them toward the second-floor stairs. Then, to his brother, 'No one follows me, Sid.'

Kling touched Dave's arm as if he meant to hold him. 'You get caught...'

'Not if I reach him before the deputy gets set. Dammit, I wouldn't be doin' this if you'd done your job last night.'

He was through the doorway and outside. The door shut in Kling's face. The trail boss didn't like the way everything had gone. The foolish shooting of Rollins that had tied him to it, Bol's trying to kill Lonergan last night and getting back with only his leg grazed, and now the inquest being held over and Dave going after Hollis. The punchers lined two deep along the counter, boots hooked onto the brass, and gave him careful, sideways stares that became more direct the more they drank. Only a few drinks, he'd told them. They were

127

too pent up, too ready to bust wide open after the long, hard cattle drive. He didn't know if he could hold them in until the inquest was finished.

Kate Morrow had the bottle and glasses he'd sent her for, and she motioned with the liquor toward the staircase. 'The party's startin',' she laughed. 'Come on, honey, we'll miss some of it.'

'Go ahead. I'll be with you in a minute.'

One of the girls was waving to Chingo Hobb from the upper railing of the stairs. 'They want us up there,' Kate added. 'Every bottle will be empty by the time we get there.'

Kling turned on her and snapped, 'Go up yourself. You want to stay with me, do what you're told.'

The smile on Kate's face vanished. The complete change made her rouged cheeks whiten; hurt and fear made her seem ridiculously childlike in her low-cut, fringed yellow dress. She nodded and hurried to the stairs.

Sid said, 'It can't go like this, Chet. Unless them deputies have enough to keep them busy, Dave could walk into real trouble.'

Kling shook his head. 'I don't want to chance a spite vote. Not only Dave they'll take in. I'm not clear either.'

'You'll get out of it once Dave's back.' Sid

128

glanced away and called down the bar. 'Set up for everyone, Dobie. I'm payin' for this one.'

'No, hold it,' Kling said. 'They drink slow. 'Til this is over, they do.'

Sid grinned, yet there was no mirth to his swollen, bruised mouth. 'You can't be held. Dave did the shootin'.' His wave included the bartender and the men pressed close at the bar. 'C'mon, drink up. Chugalug there. Chingo! Mac! You're slowin' down.'

Chingo and McGuire tilted their glasses, but most of the cowhands stayed quiet and continued to sip their shots.

Sid grinned at them and took a bottle Dobie had set on the counter. He jerked it toward the second floor. Loud, rough laughter of men, and the softer laughs and giggling of the saloon girls came through the open doorways. 'We been on the trail more than three months. We deserve a little blow-off. Hell, Chet, this town asked us to come. They ain't gonna do any turnin' if we cut up a little.'

'That's right,' Dobie laughed. 'Drink plenty. I brought a lot in here for you men you ain't used. Don't waste it.'

'We won't,' Kling said. 'There's time.'

'I'm gonna drink,' said Sid. His smile was harder, his gaze more watchful of the other cowhands. He raised the bottleneck high and downed a long swallow of whiskey. Then he

129

wiped his mouth with the sleeve of his shirt. 'You're worryin' more 'bout your own skin than you are 'bout Dave.'

'Look, I didn't want Bol callin' Lonergan. I told him.'

'You told, Kling? You were through tellin' us anythin' when you paid us off this mornin'.' Sid's stare flashed around the room and caught the mood of the listening, watchful men. 'You don't give a damn about Bol or Dave. I don't give a damn about you.'

Kling edged away from the counter until he was clear of Chingo and Sid. In the street, he'd felt this coming, in the way Dave and Sid had watched Lonergan while they'd lifted their dead brother. Damn Lonergan. Damn him! This whole thing never would have been forced to a point without him. Not to this. Kling flexed the fingers of his gunhand. 'You don't tear up. After the inquest you can have this town. You can gun down Lonergan. But not until I get that check back from the sheriff. You got that?'

Eleven cattlehands had left the brass rail and counter to move close to Kling. Now a twelfth joined them. Two more shifted their stance slightly, staying at the edge of those who backed the trail boss. Greg Connolly stepped around McGuire and Chingo Hobb and walked to Kling's side. That made it fifteen guns.

Sid studied them and was aware that only Chingo and McGuire had stayed with him. He raised the bottle again and drank long. There was no smile on his face when he handed Chingo the whiskey. Kate Morrow was looking down from the second floor. She'd been watching since Kling had made his stand. Two of the other Texans who'd been on the drive with the trail boss waited beside her.

'What you say,' Sid told Kling. He nodded toward the landing and clapped Chingo on the shoulder. 'Party's upstairs. Plenty to do while we're waitin'.'

The huge man and McGuire started for the staircase. Sid paused after them long enough to look directly into Kling's eyes. 'We've lost enough here,' he said quietly. 'Dave better get back. You cause anythin' there, you'll learn you can become just as big a target in this town as that damned fool Lonergan.'

*   *   *

Lonergan thought he heard a shout outside in the street. He turned his head to look through the curtained windows of the doctor's office.

'Stay still,' the doctor said. 'I have to get this bandage on good and tight.'

'Doctor, thanks. That's fine, just fine.'

'You want me to finish this? You don't, speak up. It's all right with me.' He straightened his thin body and stared toward the street over his steel-rimmed glasses. 'I don't know what's coming. All the time yelling and noise and trouble.'

He had the bandage tight and firm, making the shoulder feel strong, without the slightest trace of pain. Lonergan stood and was taking his shirt from the back of his chair when the bell sounded on the front porch. The sharp jingle kept up even after the doctor called he was coming. Buttoning the shirt, Lonergan moved to the window.

Boys made the commotion. Two of them ran into Frontier yelling ahead of them; the third shouted just as loud to the doctor as he opened the door.

'Mr. Hollis! He's been beaten bad! In his barn! They found him in there and they think he's dead!'

Lonergan was through the front hallway and outside behind the doctor. Shouts from Frontier were still shrill and confused. Calls from men and women who'd left their homes were as high-pitched, then more frenzied; the words became clearer the moment they turned in across the Hollis' side lawn.

'Get those people back,' the doctor shouted to the first man they passed. 'The children.

132

Keep them back.'

'Hey, you kids, don't go in there! Do what the doctor wants!'

Lonergan could see Janet Duncan beyond the open barn doorway. She leaned over low to the ground, shaking her head while she spoke to two men and a woman beside her. Neighbors stood just outside the door, talking in whispers; and most of the men lined awkwardly, waiting to help, yet not quite sure how they could. Children bounced back and forth behind their parents and made attempts to peer past them. One boy had climbed onto the shoulders of another, and the one on the bottom was complaining for his turn to see.

'Let Doc through,' said a thin young man wearing a deputy's star on his shirt. He shoved an onlooker aside with the stock of the Spencer carbine he carried. 'Let him in here.'

'I want room, Brad,' the doctor asked. 'Don't let them crowd in.'

'Doc, I found him. I was watchin' the house from the front like Ernie told me. I come 'round to check the yard, and he was layin' like that.'

'Just move them. Keep the doorway clear.'

The woman beside Janet Duncan tried to take Janet's arm, but she wouldn't let her. A buggy waited at the rear of the short aisle; a sleek-looking mare was hitched and ready to go. A shiny leather suitcase lay open near Hollis. Its contents—shirts and socks, a woman's skirt and blouse, and a boy's trousers and underclothing—were scattered in the dust.

'They were plannin' on leavin',' the deputy said. 'He'd come out and hitched up. He did it quick 'cause I was only out front five, six minutes.'

Doctor Kanter had placed the palm of his hand against the side of James Hollis' neck. He felt for a pulse before he changed the facedown position. The victim's head was resting on bits of straw that had sifted to the ground from the mow. No marks showed on his shirt or back. When the doctor knelt and carefully turned him over, Lonergan could see the blood which had seeped from his nose and mouth. It looked black in the barn's deep shadows. Hollis' head was hatless, his face still twisted with shock or pain, or both.

Ernie Loomis' voice came from above them. 'Brad, how'd this happen? You were supposed to be guardin' the house!'

'That was your job.' Judge Roddy, puffing and wheezing from his run, stepped in opposite Lonergan. His long exhaled breath blended with the gasps and short moans of the other watchers. 'Doc, that wasn't all done just now.'

The opening of the first button on the shirt beneath the dead man's coat had showed a white bandage completely encircling his chest and ribs. Lonergan watched Janet Duncan. She'd been crying but her face was now pale and composed. For a moment they stared at each other in silence. A tense, pitiful hush came over the barn and the yard.

James Hollis' entire mid-section was one swollen red and purple-black bruise. The left rib casing bulged almost twice its normal size. Low whispered talk began and stopped as quickly when the doctor finished undoing the bandage. A young Mexican laborer from the section crossed himself and mumbled a prayer. Another man muttered, 'It isn't worth it. Not this . . . damn, damn.' Others began to voice their feelings.

Lonergan said quietly to Janet, 'Did you see anyone?'

She shook her head. 'I was in the house. When I saw the deputy open the door wide.' She stopped and struggled to control herself. 'He didn't even call. I didn't hear him call.'

'He was in pain in court. Who did it?'

Again her head shook, not in refusal, but as if in disbelief at what had happened.

'Janet?' the judge said.

She looked at Lonergan. 'The gunman you shot. Jellison. He broke into the house last

135

night and beat James to make him promise he wouldn't testify. Kling and another cowboy were outside watching for him.'

'They wanted him to lie in court,' the judge said.

'There was no need to. No reason to do that to him. We couldn't see Rollins' face if he did yell. We didn't hear him.' She stared down at her brother, her small mouth distorted with emotion.

'He was going to leave? You were?'

'He was afraid. We would have wired you from Omaha.' Her head moved from side to side slowly.

Lonergan said, 'In the house, Judge. Ask her in there.'

Angry voices rose against Loomis. 'You heard her, Ernie. That trail boss was in on it. You get him.'

'Dangit, Loomis, we were warned. The Council wouldn't listen, but you should take hold now.'

Lonergan was through the crowd a step ahead of Janet and the judge. Lonnie Duncan waited at the back porch with a man and a woman. He left them and ran to his mother. Circling both arms around her waist, he held tight and looked confusedly, hopefully, into her face. 'They hurt Uncle Jimmy, Mom? Mr. Paparo said he's hurt.'

'I'll tell you inside, dear.' She gripped the boy's shoulder and started to turn him.

Lonergan said, 'Judge, do you have a crew out to your ranch? Enough to watch Lonnie?'

'I have eight men with my foreman.'

'Then I think it would be better if he stayed there.' Then he said to Janet, 'Until this is over, he'll be safer away from town.'

Janet studied him, searching the planes of his sunburned face. Her hand trembled on her son's shoulder. 'I don't ... yes, if it'll be safer.'

'I want to stay here, Mom.' Lonnie's eyes roamed across the yard to the knot of people around his uncle. 'Mom?'

'You should go with the judge,' Lonergan said. 'It'll help your mother.'

'But I want to be here.' The boy watched him, fought back the tears. 'I know what's happened. I can help.'

He looked from Lonergan to his mother. She seemed to be on the verge of speaking, but she remained silent. Lonergan glanced toward the side lawn. Sheriff Loomis had been overtaken near the street by some town businessmen and had stopped while they talked.

Lonergan squatted on his heels beside the boy. He knew how Lonnie felt. When these things happened to someone so young it was extra hard. A few years older, it might be easier. He could only try to help a little.

'Your mother shouldn't have to worry about you until after the inquest. It'll be easier for her.'

Lonnie pressed close to Lonergan, yet he wouldn't look at him. He stared at the ground and listened.

'I'll come out and get you afterward.' Lonergan squeezed one small shoulder and rose to his feet. His throat was tight as he watched the boy and the woman.

'He'll be all right. Good boy like him.' He nodded at Janet. 'I'll be waiting when the deputy takes you to the inquest tomorrow. Things will go all right.'

He moved away from them and walked to intercept the doctor coming from the barn. 'That beating Hollis took last night was a part of this just now?' Lonergan asked.

The doctor nodded. 'I'd say a rib was broken last night, and he was hit so hard today it punctured an internal organ. I'll have to make an autopsy before I can be definite.'

'Thank you. For everything, Doc.' He glanced at Janet Duncan and her son going into the house with the judge. He breathed in deeply and thought of what she'd said to him about his bringing the trouble. Up until this minute, he'd depended too much on Loomis.

The sight of Hollis' viciously bruised body was too fresh in his mind; the knowledge of what could come to Janet and her son, too plain. He had the right to apply his own pressure now.

And he knew exactly where he would start.

*　　*　　*

'He's been in my place all mornin',' Jonas Dobie was telling Loomis. 'I'll swear in court Kling hasn't left my place.'

'So you let him alone,' Arthur Dexter put in. 'You've made enough mess of the trouble, Ernie. Don't make another mistake.'

'Damned right,' said a third town merchant. 'You want the sheriff's appointment. Use your head.' He crowded the lawman with the others who'd stopped him on the sidewalk and who now stood blocking him from going back onto Frontier. Loomis faced them, looking at their open coats; each was showing heavy gold watch chains and diamond stick pins, the stamps of hard-won success exposed to him as a sign of importance and power.

'You know you can wait, Ernie. Just 'til mornin'. We planned everythin' so the trail crew would do business here. Not one of them has as much as been near a store. We've got to

139

give them time.'

The sheriff flicked his tongue over his lips. 'Kling was there when Hollis was beaten last night.'

'He didn't do the beatin',' Dobie said. He looked toward his saloon and listened to the piano music that had started again. The windows on the second floor had been opened, the blinds thrown high, and they all could see the figures of men and women move back and forth in the rooms. Laughter and talk, if there was any, was so low and controlled it didn't even sound in the street. 'Kling's holdin' them down. He didn't do the actual beatin'.'

Ernie Loomis saw Lonergan step into the crowd and work his way through to the middle. Again the lawman shook his head, as if he tried to shake off an annoying fly.

'Mr. Dobie, unless we have law and order, we'll lose more than we gain.'

'Sheriff, you know who helped beat James Hollis,' Lonergan said. 'Are you going to take Kling in?'

Lowney from the Goodland Hotel spoke quickly. 'We've discussed that. Kling didn't do the actual beating.'

'Sheriff?' Lonergan repeated. Then, when Ernie Loomis didn't answer, he added, 'I was offered a badge in this town. In a letter, and inside the cattle office yesterday.'

'No, you aren't the one we want,' Dobie said with a note of shrillness. 'Not now, we don't need you.'

Lonergan stared from face to face and met the businessmen's eyes: Dexter, Lowney, Dobie, Fullerton. One or two glanced away and wouldn't look at him. A sudden outbreak of laughter bounced through the open windows of the saloon. A woman's high-pitched mock scream came, and subsided under louder, rougher laughter and talk.

'A man was beaten to death, Sheriff,' Lonergan said. 'The law is the only way. A good, strong law.'

'That's not you,' Dobie said. 'We told you.'

'It isn't your business,' said Fullerton. 'The man who tried killing you was a Jellison. That was your own personal trouble.'

Lonergan waited for the sheriff, who peered at the moving figures in the Drovers Bar upper floor windows. The shouts and yells and noisy laughter grew louder and wilder.

'Jellison was with that crew,' Lonergan stated flatly. He took a first step toward the intersection. 'They are my trouble.'

'Well, dammit,' a man sputtered. 'What's he doin'?'

'Who in hell he think he is?' Dobie said. He shuffled his feet and watched Lonergan. 'He barges in my place, I'll turn my scattergun on him. Ernie?'

Ernie Loomis paused a fraction of a second longer, enough to throw a hasty look at Dexter and Lowney and Fullerton. Then, elbows and arms moving, he hurried through the crowd to catch up with Lonergan.

CHAPTER TWELVE

Lonergan heard Ernie Loomis call his name, but he kept up his fast stride into Goodland's main street.

The heavy thump of the lawman's boots was close behind him, then alongside. 'I'm wearin' the badge, Lonergan. I'll say what goes.'

'Then have your say. Janet Duncan and her son could be next if you don't.'

'Kling didn't come out. They might not even know about Hollis.'

'They know. Every last one of them knows.' Lonergan watched the building's windows, doorways, the alleyways. Just a single member of the trail crew was in sight outside the saloon, a tall cowhand with his horse in the work area of the livery. The husky, leather-aproned blacksmith and the

142

cowhand both glanced up from the horseshoe that seemed to be giving trouble.

The cattle train backed to the middle of the siding was almost completely loaded. The redwood water tank stood like a silent sentinel guarding the graze area and the bluish-gray of the Platte. Only the slight off-water breeze, puffing up small gusts of dust where the horses tied at the hitchrails kicked or shifted on the dirt gave any real motion to the town. This lack of movement accented the irony of the day's quiet heat and masked the seething hate and violence of James Hollis' death. Lonergan's right hand tightened his gunbelt and raised the butt of his .44 Colt so the palm brushed the solid wood.

'I'll do the talkin',' Loomis said. 'Let me.'

'Do your job, Sheriff, nobody'll have to step in.'

Loomis glanced across his shoulder at Lowney, Fullerton, and Dexter, who were following with Jonas Dobie. Lonergan had been aware of them and of the other men, and a few boys, barely high school age, hanging behind them. More of the Texas trail crew were in the stores than he'd first thought. One came out onto the mercantile porch. Two of them, with a pair of Dobie's girls, paused going up the front steps of the hotel. No one spoke a word while the saloon owner left the

143

group to run ahead of Lonergan and the sheriff and reach the Drovers' batwings before them.

Eight of Kling's riders were lined along the saloon bar. Three sat at a wall table under the stuffed heads of buffalo and an elk, playing Red Dog with Dobie's dealer. Dobie hurried behind the counter to his handyman and spoke quickly to him. The handyman, years older than the saloon owner, had white, silky hair. He was short and narrow, and so round-shouldered that he had to lift his head to stare from the sheriff and Lonergan past the stuffed trophies to the polished rails of the staircase and the landing. The strumming of a guitar, accompanied by singing, could be heard from upstairs, but the song was dulled because two of the three doors were closed.

The handyman took a damp towel from beneath the bar and began to edge toward the stairs while he mopped the mahogany.

'Stay down here,' Lonergan said.

Dobie swore softly. 'Look, Ernie, you can see nothin's goin' on.'

Loomis walked straight to the counter. Lonergan halted a full stride behind the lawman at the corner of the gilt-edged mirror. He could see Dexter and Lowney and Fullerton step inside together. Two more town merchants and the husky blacksmith were with them. Those who'd followed hung back outside the double doors. Men peered through the window and over the batwings and small boys had crawled under the slatted doors to watch.

The cowhands had stopped their talk. A rangy, blond Texan wearing a flat Spanish sombrero touched the man next to him. As the word traveled to the tables, all heads turned. Loomis stood without speaking. He glanced from face to face, then switched his stare to the landing.

Dobie said again, 'You can see, Ernie. Take Lonergan out of here and don't let him push you into trouble.'

The rangy man in the Spanish sombrero grinned, took a whiskey-filled shot glass and held it out to Loomis. 'Have a drink, Sheriff. C'mon. First one's on Dobie.'

Loomis made no move to accept the offer. 'Any of these men go out of here in the past half hour?' he asked the handyman.

The white-haired head shook. 'No. They all been right here.'

'How about the ones upstairs.'

'They all been right in here.' Nervously, he eyed the cattlehands. Some were smiling; one was downing his liquor. They looked as if they'd been drinking slowly and carefully; they bent over their whiskey and beer with little movement showing except in the slits of their eyes or a hand fingering a glass or a bottle.

Loomis said, 'James Hollis was found beaten to death in his barn.' The grin on the blond's face faded. Smiles vanished along the bar, at the tables.

One of the men spoke gravely. 'You ain't blamin' us, Sher'ff. We been right in here, like he says.' He glanced from the handyman to the stairs. 'You heard him say so.'

Dexter said, 'You've no right taking anyone in. Not with all these witnesses.'

'How about upstairs?' Lonergan said. 'There's a staircase leading from the end of the hall outside.'

'Dammit,' said Fullerton. 'You touch one of them, Ernie, they can sue for false arrest. They have enough witnesses.'

Lonergan edged away from Ernie Loomis; he expected the lawman to move. The sheriff eyed Dexter and Fullerton in the mirror. His right hand twitched and he ended the flutter by rubbing it along his pantsleg. He stepped out in front of Lonergan and climbed the stairs.

Chet Kling appeared in the open doorway before they reached the landing. He was sweating, his face flushed from dancing and liquor. He broke into a happy grin and said,

146

'Hello, Sheriff. We haven't been makin' too much noise?'

'No, you haven't,' Dobie said quickly. 'I told them you were holdin' your men quiet. We couldn't even hear you downstairs.'

'Then you come for a drink.' Kling gestured behind him to Kate Morrow, Lew, Sid, and the other cattlehands and women who edged back to let Ernie Loomis into the room. His grin broadened, moved past Lonergan as if he weren't there, and took in the town businessmen. 'Give them a drink. They been workin' hard fixin' up for us. Give them all a drink.'

Most of the cowhands and saloon women laughed. Only Sid and Lew, and Dave at the very rear of the room, did not laugh. The three were silent and apart from the celebration; every bit of their attention was centered on Lonergan.

'James Hollis was found dead in his barn just now.' Loomis picked out the women, and nodded to one, then another, and finally to Kate Morrow. 'Did anyone leave these rooms?'

Chet Kling said, 'No one's left this shindig. Sheriff, we agreed to stay quiet 'til the inquest is finished.' He shook his head. 'You don't know what it's like to hold this crew down.'

Lonergan said, 'The sheriff asked Kate.

147

She can answer for herself.'

'Dammit, Loomis, keep him shut,' said Dobie. 'I don't want him in here causin' trouble.'

'He's pushin' you, Ernie,' Lowney added. 'You heard them downstairs.'

Loomis nodded at Kate. 'You've been in here right along?'

Kate Morrow tugged at the bodice of her dress, pulling it up higher on the shoulders. 'I couldn't see what went on in or out.'

Kling had circled his arm around her. She let him hold her and snuggled against him. He smiled down at her; his broad, hard grin was very personal now. 'How could we see. We been so busy. Dobie'd seen if anybody left, not us.'

'Yes,' Kate said. 'Mr. Dobie would've seen.'

'Dobie couldn't watch the upstairs door,' Lonergan told her.

'Well, I didn't see anyone leave or come in.' Kate visibly relaxed as Kling loosened his grip. She backed away and watched the men's expressions. Her face was white under the rouge; her hands were together nervously over the deep V of her dress. 'I can't say one thing. I can't.'

'Yeah, we'll be witnesses for each other,' a thin, raw-boned cowhand said. 'Everyone of

148

us in here, Sheriff.' Male and female voices spoke loudly, their statements confused and noisy, but all agreeing.

'Loomis, can't you see?' Art Dexter said. 'You'd waste your time. The judge wouldn't even hold one of them with so much backin'.'

Loomis paused, a bit unsure. Dobie said, 'The judge was knockin' on doors, Ernie. He's got enough with the inquest.' He started to turn toward the hall and staircase. 'Let these men . . .'

'Hollis was given a beating last night,' Lonergan said. 'You were there, Kling.' He watched the sheriff. 'We've got a witness to that.'

'I damnwell was,' Kling admitted. 'That Jellison you killed did it. But I didn't lay a hand on Hollis. Lew'll back me on that. I waited outside and let Bol do his own work.'

'That's right,' Lew said. 'I was outside, too. Bol tried to talk to Hollis and he went crazy. He went for a carbine on his fireplace.' His speech was run together drunkenly, but he knew exactly how his roughness and ugly look affected the Goodland merchants. 'You promised us a big time. This what you call a good time, havin' your law keep on us every minute?'

Muttering and mumbling rose from the cowhands. 'Damn rotten place,' remarked one puncher. 'We drove the extra distance, this is what we get.' Chingo Hobb moved his huge bulk in against Kling's shoulder. 'You figure we're goin' to want to make another drive, you're dead wrong. Sheriff, you take Chet, the only money this town'll see is what's paid for the booze.'

Dobie said, 'No, you'll see we mean what we promised. The check Kling gave is enough for this, too. It won't be handed over 'til this is settled, but that's enough.' Lowney, Dexter, and Fullerton nodded briskly, and waited for Loomis.

Lonergan watched the sheriff. He knew the lawman had lost every last bit of intent and drive he'd had outside in the street. He was sick of the whole cover-up and what went on in here—the flushed sweaty faces, the mixed, heady odors of cattle, unwashed bodies, liquor, and cheap perfume.

'I'll know where to come,' the lawman said to Kling. He rubbed his fleshy jowls and met the trail boss' direct stare. 'Don't leave town. I'll put out a dodger.'

'I'll be right here.' Kling reached for a bottle, raised it to his lips, and tilted his head far back while he swallowed. Some whiskey spilled, but he simply wiped it with the sleeve of his shirt.

In the rising talk and laughter, Kate

Morrow took a step away from Kling. She was near the doorway behind the departing men when the trail boss realized she'd moved. He went after her.

Kling grabbed her arm and swung her around. 'What you tryin'?'

'Lonergan'll keep after Loomis. If I can talk to him.'

Kling threw her backward and slammed her against Sid, who was directly behind him. 'Stay in here. Right here.' Kate uttered a shocked, pained gasp. She was grabbed by Chingo and Lew and pushed roughly through to the rear of the gathering. Lonergan had halted and turned to face Kling.

'She had something to say,' Lonergan began.

'Not to you. You'll be busy enough with the Jellisons.'

Lonergan's eyes flicked beyond the main room. Kate was lost from sight, pushed from hand to hand among the bodies. 'Do that to me,' he said.

'You need it, damn you,' Kling blurted. He crouched and raised the whiskey bottle. Lonergan's open hand slammed out, the solid bone of the knuckles hitting Kling flush on the jaw so fast and so violently that the trail boss reeled back against his cowhands.

Lonergan caught Sid's hand as it started to

sweep down for his holster. Lonergan's Colt was out and cocked while it leveled off belt high; the long, silver barrel was ready before the other weapon could clear leather.

Sid froze. Lonergan held the sixgun poised. His hand shook. He stared at them, let them see the hand and the tight smile that cracked his lips.

'You come that close,' he said, his gray eyes flashing cold. 'That close. You think you can ruin so many lives.' He studied the faces, watching Sid and Lew more than the others. 'Keep after a man, you'll force him to decide. It won't be this pretty.'

He backstepped into the hallway and closed the door.

Sid cursed. He headed for the hallway, his hand on his sixgun.

Lew grabbed him. 'Not like that. Not in the back.'

'I'm goin' to get him!'

'You will. Get these men to act up, we will. Dammit, Kling.'

Kling stood flat on both feet, got his balance, and rubbed one hand along the ugly red welt that swelled his jawline. His voice was hoarse, showing the effect of the blow. He scanned the roomful of men, his eyes dark and furious. 'We held the noise down so there'd be no trouble. Well, you're a cattle crew, and this stinkin' town made us promises. You have your fun.'

Shouts went up, wild rebel yells and curses. Bottles were passed around; corks were popped out of unopened liquor. Women squealed happily and returned to the men; Kate Morrow was among them. She smiled unsteadily at Kling and wasn't quite sure what to do.

'I wanted to tell him you'd been in here. Right in here,' she offered. 'Honest, Chet.'

Masssaging his jawbone, Kling glared at her.

'She damnwell wanted to do more,' Sid said. 'You saw that.'

A cowhand on the opposite corner of the room was swearing wildly. 'I c'n beat you,' he shouted. 'My horse'll beat yours any time, any day!'

'Hell it can,' another argued. He raised the bottle he'd emptied above his head and hurled it through the window into the street. 'The hell you can!'

Kate Morrow placed one hand timidly on Chet Kling's forearm. 'You've been good to me.' She was pale; every trace of the liquor she'd had was gone in her sobering fear. 'He'd find a way to blame you for Hollis. He would, Chet. I don't want to lose you.'

Chet Kling turned away from her. He

153

jerked his wrist free of her hand. 'You'll stay here,' he said. 'But not with me. Sid. Chingo.'

'Chet, please.' She tried to move around in front of him. He shook her off with a twist of his shoulders. Chingo's big hand took hold of her arm. 'Chet, please! Please!'

'Take her, Chingo.'

Chingo grinned, a wide, ugly smile. 'She'll stay shut. I know a way.'

Kling drew a deep breath, conscious of the noise and confusion in every corner of the room. Three more men had circled in close to Chingo and the girl. 'See she's shut,' he said in a hard, empty voice. 'I want a drink.'

'Chet, I want you, only you,' Kate pleaded. Chingo's strong fingers dragged her back. Nodding to the men near him, and for the women to stay clear, he picked a full whiskey bottle from the table and shoved Kate toward the adjoining room.

'She'll stay shut. She'll be damned sorry she even tried to get out and talk up to Lonergan.'

CHAPTER THIRTEEN

Lonergan knew he had been wrong a second time.

He'd halted halfway across Frontier after

154

leaving the saloon and had expected Sid and Lew to come after him. They were Jellisons, he was sure now. And maybe the one called Dave... Yet, he'd been as mistaken about being followed as he'd been in believing that Loomis would make a firm stand inside the room.

The sheriff hadn't gone into his office but had spotted himself on the jail walk. He watched Lonergan and the saloon doors as closely as Lonergan did. The two young deputies he'd sworn in waited alongside him, long-barreled Spencer carbines in their hands, listening to Judge Roddy and the town businessmen, who were all keeping after Loomis.

Loomis nodded to Dexter's quick words, but didn't even glance at him. 'Lonergan,' he said. 'You haven't got a room to stay. I know a house.'

'He'll have a place.' Judge Roddy stared toward the noise and shouts that poured out of the broken upstairs saloon window. Then a second of the four large panes had crashed outward. Wood, glass, and putty, and the chair that had been thrown sprayed everything within thirty feet. A man and a woman who'd been walking past had to rush off the planks and go along the middle of the roadway to escape the debris.

'See,' the judge said. 'They'll tear this town apart if you don't hold them down.'

Dexter grinned from Lowney to Fullerton. 'A couple windows. Dobie'll take care of that.'

'It'll spread,' said Lonergan. 'I've seen these trail crews turn a town inside out once they go.'

'I warned them,' said the judge. 'This was all hashed out at council meeting. A town can become a shipping center without offering something like this.'

'Hell,' Fullerton told them. 'They ain't doin' any real harm. They'll blow off their steam and turn in. Lowney's already got half his rooms rented. The rest'll be bringin' in the remuda Kling's sellin' me.' War whoops and yells cut off his words as the third window splintered with a loud crash onto the porch roof, and showered the walk and street. 'Dobie's already agreed to stand any cost like that. Some of us'll kick in too.' ·

'Sure we will,' Lowney agreed. He was looking at the faces that peered down at them from his hotel windows—cowhands and two of Dobie's women, laughing, guzzling the whiskey they held. 'We'll carry the load.'

Judge Roddy shook his head, his anger reddening his deep-lined skin. 'You already have two men dead. You have to put a guard on Janet Duncan and send her boy out of

156

town, and you still refuse to face the fact that you've got trouble.'

'That came from him.' Lowney pointed directly at Lonergan. 'Rollins wouldn't have crossed Kling if he hadn't been in that office arguin' about his cows.'

'Damn right,' Dexter added. 'Ernie can hold anything in hand. He did up in that room. He's got deputies now.'

Ernie Loomis nodded and said to the deputies, 'Brad you take the east end. Walt, the west end and stock pens. Keep the women and kids out of the way 'til the riders settle down.'

While Loomis stepped into his office and the deputies started off, Dexter, Lowney, and the other town merchants moved toward their stores and businesses.

'I don't know,' said Judge Roddy, shaking his head. 'For the few dollars they'll take in ... They all have children who'll have to pick up the bad that comes.'

Lonergan didn't answer. If any attack had been held off because the lawmen stayed outside, it could come now. The sun, dropping toward the timber that blocked a full view of the Platte, moved behind a line of whitish clouds, partially veiling its glare. Longer shadows slanting east made the day more subdued, yet the raucous wildness took all that away. Two cattlehands came out of the saloon with a pair of Dobie's girls. The shorter, a roundish, lardy man, spotted Lonergan and the judge. He waved his bottle in the air and called something they couldn't make out clearly while he went up the hotel steps.

Judge Roddy took a key from his pocket. 'My office is on the second floor over the court. There's a daybed I use. It'll be enough for the night.'

'I'll be a witness tomorrow, Judge. They could claim I'm too close to you.'

'Let them claim what they want.'

'Watch it.' Lonergan had sidestepped clear of him at the sudden appearance of five men shoving out past the Drovers' batwings. More men and two of the saloon women crowded the open second-floor windows. Lonergan relaxed again and watched the five untie their horses. They were arguing and cursing loudly and obscenely. They climbed into their saddles, spurred the animals, and galloped across the intersection into Cross Street.

Judge Roddy placed the key in Lonergan's palm. 'Janet said for you to use her barn for your horse.' And when he thought that Lonergan might refuse, he said, 'You can't leave him in the open. Use her barn. It'll help her to know someone's near. Whoever killed her brother won't be so quick to bother her if they know you're around.'

Lonergan slipped the key into his shirt pocket and crossed Frontier to the jail hitchrails. He had the halter knot undone, but he didn't raise his boot to the stirrup. The riders had whirled their horses at the north end of Cross. They bellowed out whooping yells and raced back along the roadway, their mounts galloping at breakneck speed. Cowhands and their women shouted and cheered from the saloon porch and windows. Dobie, at the edge of the top step, held up a whiskey bottle for the winner.

Lonergan led his stallion on the bridle across the walk and looked over his shoulder before he stepped into the alley. He couldn't pick out Sid or Lew among the throng on the Drovers' porch—or Kling and the man called Dave. The five horsemen charged toward Dobie, taking swipes at each other with their sombreros, their horses' flanks rubbing, rumps banging, crowded together into the street's narrowness. That and the pitch of the screams and yells made a deep, icy shiver run through him. It wasn't fear, but a sense of what could come with the wildness unleashed.

They'd hooraw Goodland. Loomis, his deputies, and the town businessmen couldn't picture how it could be—like huge immense rocks that had suddenly come loose and rolled and crashed down a hillside with nothing to stop them or turn them aside until they'd completely run their course . . .

★   ★   ★

He was forking hay into the bin for the black when he heard the rear door of the house open. He had finished rubbing down the horse and had led the stallion into the first stall to settle him for the night. Janet Duncan came off the porch stairs. She seemed tired and small as she walked through the thickening shade of the yard. The soft slenderness of her features and the calm and control of her walk made her quiet loveliness blend in with the beauty of the prairie afternoon.

He leaned the pitchfork against the stall beam and walked up the aisle to meet her.

'I'm glad Judge Roddy had you bring your horse,' she said, 'I wanted you to.'

'I'll handle your mare. The judge'll know someone around town who'll be able to keep things right for you.'

'No, Lonnie can hitch the buggy.'

'There'll be more that could be done by a handyman.'

'We won't need one,' she said. 'We're

leaving after the inquest.' She gazed beyond him to the spot where her brother had been found and she rubbed her cheek with her fingers. The faint coolness of the river breeze touched her hair, blowing a few strands loose along her forehead. She brushed them back. 'You helped with Lonnie, and I want to thank you. You haven't asked anything since you've come. I was wrong.'

'It doesn't matter, Janet.' Taking her arm, he turned her from the barn and walked her toward the house.

'Yes, I think it does. You tried to give James the right advice. You didn't have to take the time with my son.'

'If you'd only told the judge about the beating.'

'James didn't trust the protection Loomis gave us. All Bol Jellison had to do last night was kick our lock open to get at us.'

She moved her head slowly around to look at the barn. Her face was drawn now, very pale and very tired. 'He thought if we reached Omaha we could have more protection. He was more worried about Lonnie and me.' She was silent a moment as she listened to an outbreak of shouting in the business district. The sound of another window being broken was followed by gales of shouts and laughter. 'He believed in the promise of Goodland,' she

continued. 'That a name could be made...
The price of a man's life.'

Lonergan touched her arm gently. She
straightened her shoulders. 'I'm all right,' she
said, not taking her eyes from the open barn
doorway. 'James was all we had when I lost
my husband. He asked for a transfer from the
main office to give Lonnie the chance to grow
up outside a large city.'

'He still can. He'll be safe at the judge's.
And after...'

His words broke off as suddenly as she'd
gripped his hand. They'd both seen the
brighter flash of afternoon daylight show
inside the barn. A shadowy form moved into
the barn; then the light was gone.

'Inside,' Lonergan said. He kept his
attention on Janet long enough to know she'd
opened the porch door and closed it behind
her.

Circling wide to the left, he drew his Colt.
He held it cocked and aimed while he
flattened his body against the building's rough
boards and inched toward the open doorway.

CHAPTER FOURTEEN

Lonergan didn't move for many moments, but stared into what he could see of the front stalls. He had no idea who had come into the barn, nor did he have any illusions about Janet Duncan or himself. Testimony she'd give would be made to stand up by Judge Roddy. Feeling against him was strong in Goodland. The powers of the town as well as the Jellisons and the trail crew hated him. If either he or Janet were killed it would settle a lot of problems that had come since yesterday afternoon.

'Lonergan? You there, Lonergan?'

A small form, hunched low against the sideboards of the last stall, was visible now. He edged in closer, the Colt ready, his finger taut on the trigger. He could make out the thin, oval face of Kate Morrow, her body pressed against the wood, using it for support.

Relief made his stomach weak. He slid the sixgun into its holster and stepped inside to the woman.

'I knew you'd led your horse back here,' the saloon girl said. She didn't straighten from her hunched position. 'I knew I'd find you.'

'What's the matter, Kate?'

163

She swayed toward him, and he caught her by the shoulders, surprised to feel how thin and frail she actually was. 'Easy. Take it easy. Easy.'

'I'll be fine in a minute,' she said, giving him a smile. The grin was all wrong, as mistaken and meaningless as her attempt to stand without his help. She looked ghastly in the little light; her mouth was swollen along her bitten lips; the rouge of both cheeks was smeared and streaked down along her jaws and neckline.

'Keep leaning on my arm. What happened?'

'Chet Kling let me go,' she said. 'I'm so smart. I pick out the strong one in any cattle crew. Chet gave me to Chingo Hobb.' She shook her head quickly and grimaced; the smeared makeup dug into the lines of her jaw. 'They thought I was tryin' to tell somethin'. The brute, the way he ... He beat me, did this to me.'

Lonergan tightened his arm about her waist and helped her walk. 'They could have seen you come here.'

'I went out the alleyway stairs.' She halted and looked toward the rear door of the house. Janet Duncan watched through the curtained window. Kate clung to him. 'Dave Jellison won't be satisfied 'til he can't be touched.

164

That family won't stop against you.' She again stared at Janet, who had opened the door to step onto the porch. 'You're right to watch her. Keep her where she'll be safe.'

'Janet can't hurt them. Not about Rollins, or her brother. You come in. She'll help you.'

Kate Morrow stared at him and the house, and then she tried to back away. 'I don't belong in there. I wanted to tell you. We use a house in the old section.'

'You'll stay here.' He glanced at Janet coming down to them, her hands and arms raised ready to help. 'You'll be safe inside with Janet, Kate.'

*   *   *

Lew Jellison came out of the last room into the hallway, and hurried toward Dave and Kling on the landing. 'She isn't there either. Sid and Mac haven't been able to find her.'

'She was inside when I went down,' Chingo said. 'I didn't think she'd be able...'

'Shut up! Just keep shut,' Kling told him.

'You too, damn you,' Dave snapped. 'You hadn't let him have her, it wouldn't've happened.' He'd been in this exact spot for a full minute, looking down through the hazy, swirling layers of cigar and cigarette smoke. Three of Dobie's girls were at the bar; a fourth was watching the Red Dog game at a side table. Kate Morrow wasn't one of them. The noise along the bar was as loud as the hell-raising that went on in the rooms behind him.

Polson and Bonney had just about drained the bottle Lawson had won in the horse race. Half of the crew was crowded around them while they bellowed and yelled at each other in another argument. Ike Hunt and J.P. Delock talked with Dobie opposite the big, shiny mirror. Dave didn't like how MacNevin and four more of the married riders stuck to the far end of the brass rail, downing their drinks alone and taking no part in the goings-on. Their quiet and staying together could mean something. It was growing dark outside. The evening shadows stretched clear across Frontier, and the porch lights had been lit on the general store. If the family men had reached the point of leaving, not even the night could hold them.

He couldn't be positive, though. About them, or what Kate Morrow had in her mind. 'We go downstairs,' he told the others. 'Sid, you and Kling take Dobie's office. Chingo, Lew, the side storerooms.'

'Dobie wouldn't hide her,' Kling said. 'He knows we'd tear this place apart.'

Dave cursed. 'Check the rooms. Make damned sure.'

166

'She took off, I tell you,' Chingo said. 'She's gone for Lonergan. I figured she'd make a beeline for Lonergan.'

Kling said, 'You should have figured on that 'fore you left her alone. You *had* to go down after another one.'

'Dammit, don't climb on me. You gave her away. You didn't do any more figurin' than I did. You have to be in on shuttin' her up. Both her and the Duncan woman.' He'd halted at the edge of the landing and waited, ready and willing to face the trail boss in any kind of a fight.

Dave Jellison shoved Kling ahead of him and started him down the stairs. 'Get the check made, both of you. We don't shut anyone 'til we find them.'

The irritated, open stares King got from the sections of the bar and the tables were enough for Dave Jellison. And Chingo's stand against the trail boss. At mid-bar, neither Dobie nor the cowhands had as much as glanced around.

'One hundred, then,' Ike Hunt was saying to the saloon owner. 'Fifty bucks from each of us.'

'No. I have to have it shipped from Chicago,' Dobie argued good-naturedly. 'It cost me almost that much in shipping charges.'

'One hundred ten bucks,' said J.P. Delock.

He spotted Dave and he threw an arm around his shoulder. 'What you think?' he asked drunkenly. 'We offered him a bargain for the mirror there, and he won't sell.'

'So nice and gold,' Ike said. 'All that gold on the sides.'

'It's only painted,' Dobie explained, the good-natured grin still on his mouth. 'I can't sell it. I need it. I couldn't get another one for four times what they'd pay me.'

Dave laughed. 'You two'd look good tryin' to herd that mirror all the miles back to the Pecos.' He moved easily out from under Delock's arm and said to the bartender, 'Did Kate Morrow come down here?'

'I didn't see her.' Dobie gazed toward Chingo and Lew. The pair had stepped out of the storeroom and had circled the tables to meet Kling and Sid near the office. 'Look, if you think she's stole somethin', I'll take care of it.' He didn't get an answer because some of the cattle crew farther down the bar had crowded toward them, calling to him.

'You got a buggy?' one questioned. 'Barkeep, you got one you stable out in your barn?'

'Sure.' Dobie gave a small grin. 'Listen, have a bottle on the house. You've had your race.'

'Hell we have,' a second rider told him. 'My

168

horse had a loose shoe.' He waved at Dave and Kling and the rest for verification. 'We get horses and wagons from this town, they'll be fresh. I can beat this poke in a race. Any day, any time!'

The cowhands who had crowded in around them guffawed and joked and egged him on. 'Lowney'd have a wagon,' somebody said. 'I'll drive it.' Two more shoved in closer to the bar. 'The smith would have one,' another shouted. 'I'll handle that. Finch'll go see the haberdasher.'

Dobie tried to quiet them, but the shouts and talk became louder. The men were already making bets. 'I'll have my surrey horse harnessed,' he said. 'You'll be careful? You won't take any chances?'

'We'll be good 'n' careful.'

'Yah! Sure, we'll be careful. We been handlin' horses long as you been pourin' booze.'

Sid had Dave's sleeve and he backed with him and Kling toward the bar end. 'There's a house the girls use in the old section. It gets darker, we could hunt her there.'

Kling shook his head. 'Could be other girls with her.' His quick worried glance surveyed the cowhands mobbed at the center bar. 'They're too drunk. They'll kill themselves.'

'Let them go,' Dave said.

169

'They'd be better off out to the pens. They'll...' Kling's words were cut off as Dave's left hand grabbed his arm and pulled him close. Sid, Lew, even Chingo, crowded against him. No one could see the sixgun Dave had whipped out and jabbed into his stomach.

'They'll run their race,' Dave said. 'They're not leavin'. Anyone wants to leave, you talk them out of it. You better.'

'You're crazy,' Kling said.

'They keep like this,' Dave said calmly. He nodded at the noisy talk and movement; all the men and women inside the saloon joined in now. 'They'll gang up out in the street. There'll be plenty hollerin' and yellin'. It'll cover us findin' Kate and the Duncan woman and Lonergan.'

Kling saw the faint, cold smiles alongside him and felt the solid steel barrel prod deeper into his middle. He raised both of his arms and waved at his crew. 'Come on, let's hear it,' he called. 'You want a race, you'll get one. C'mon, let's hear it.'

*　　*　　*

Matt Lonergan said, 'I know it wasn't Kling in the barn the second time. Whoever did corner Janet's brother would've gone to tell

170

Kling.' He watched Kate Morrow closely. 'Try to think. Who came into the party late?'

Kate lay on the living room sofa. Lonergan had wet a towel and had cleaned the smeared rouge and makeup from her face. Strands of blonde hair fell across her damp cheek, but she didn't seem aware of that.

'So many were downstairs,' she said. 'They kept coming and going. I can't be sure.' She gave a stiff, unnatural smile to Lonergan, stared at the rifle above the stone fireplace, then looked toward the kitchen. Her smile was the kind Lonergan had seen in the eyes of women who needed to scream. She had lain like this since Janet had led her inside. Her knees were curled up as if she tried to make herself as small as possible. The lines of her body were rigid; the smooth muscles of her forearms, drawn into small knots. 'I shouldn't stay here. I should leave.'

Lonergan touched her shoulder gently. 'Stay right here. Where would you go?'

'Go?' The smile grew tighter. 'It'll be dark. There's the house at the east end.' A spasm shook her shoulders and she gripped both arms by the elbows and squeezed her body. 'You've been too nice to me. Both of you. I'll only make more trouble for you.'

'You're not making trouble. Janet said you could stay tonight. She's leaving this town and you can go on the same train.'

'I can't leave,' she said in a small, weary voice. 'I owe Mr. Dobie money. He paid my fare. He paid all of our fares. He'd have me taken in.'

'He won't have you touched. He can't do one thing to you or any of the girls he brought here.'

Kate shook her head quickly, her eyes bright with fear. 'They would. To her, too, if they could.' She watched Janet Duncan come in from the kitchen with a coffee pot and three steaming mugs on the tray she carried. Lonergan handed a cup to Kate. He waited until she'd taken a sip, then said softly, 'Don't worry about Dobie. Or any of them. They won't even know where you are.'

Kate sighed. 'I don't know why Chet did that. I didn't look at any of the others. Only him. I did what he wanted at the inquest. You saw how I stood up and tried to be heard.'

'Kling told you exactly what to say?'

'He didn't have to.' Her eyes widened across the rim of the cup. 'I didn't lie. Rollins did look like he was reaching for a gun. That's what I can't understand. I helped Chet, but he still did that to me.' She shivered and sipped again. 'I didn't know they could be like ... like animals. I don't want to go back. I don't.'

Janet Duncan nodded. Both Kate and

172

Lonergan saw that, and Lonergan said, 'You were near Kling all the time. Did anyone call him aside to talk with him before we came to the hotel room? Think now.'

'He was talking to so many people. I didn't hear anyone say a word about this house.' She shook her head and looked down into the cup. Janet took the steaming pot to pour more coffee.

Lonergan motioned her away and stood over Kate, his voice and tone harder, more direct. 'Kling must have spoken to someone. He wasn't surprised when he heard who'd been killed. He'd been told.'

Kate's head began to move from side to side.

'Think. If we can have one man taken in, it's a start. They have no way of knowing you're here.'

'He did talk to Lew and Dave, and the other Jellison but I didn't hear a word they said.' There was fear in her eyes.

'Did any of them come in late?'

'I can't tell you,' she whispered. 'So many were going in and out. The other girls, too.' Her voice cracked at the last word, partly because of her emotion, but mainly because of the shot that had been fired outside in the street. More gunfire followed the first; the continuous banging was a part of the shouts and cheers that kept growing louder and louder toward the town's center.

Lonergan went into the front hall and peered out the window. A man stood on the lawn between the two houses directly opposite the window, yet he couldn't be certain about him. Despite the illumination thrown by the porch lamps, he could see very little in the rising dusk. The cheers kept up, gunfire pounded, wilder and less controlled than he'd first thought, and he could hear the rattle and rumble of wagons and the clomping of horses' hoofs. He stepped back into the parlor. Kate Morrow looked like a terrified child; she crouched almost double on the sofa, hugging herself tighter.

'They're holding a wagon race,' he told the women. 'It has nothing to do with you.'

'It could,' Kate whispered. 'If Kling or Chingo knew I came to find you.'

'You'll be all right, both of you.' He nodded to Janet and walked through to the kitchen. 'Lock the door after me.'

'They must be hunting,' she began.

'I'll see.' He turned the wick down, stepped to the door, and stood so he wouldn't show a movement behind the curtain. The yard was very dark, with only the barn roof clearly visible against the last hazy yellow and crimson light along the distant horizon.

'You know how to fire the rifle in the parlor?'

'Yes.'

'Use it if you have to. You don't have to hit anything. Just keep shooting.'

'You could stay.'

He met her direct stare, and said quietly, 'If they intend to come, I'll know. I'll be back. Just be ready.'

'I ... we will.' He couldn't see her face plainly, but against the lamp glare of the parlor he could tell the change in her whole manner. She was straight and as composed as she had been when he'd first met her. But her words were soft and showed concern for him. 'Be careful. Please. Don't worry about us.'

He went onto the stone stoop and waited only the fraction of a minute it took to hear the click of the bolt being slid into place. The shouting had grown to a rough screaming; the gun shots came faster, some on this side of the intersection. The quiet back yard didn't have a movement to it. He drew the .44 and thumbed the hammer. Keeping close to the side of the house, he hurried down the sandy lawn toward the roadway.

★　　★　　★

Front doors were opened all along the road as

families watched Cross and Frontier. The gunfire lessened and broke off to single-space shots; then only the yells and peals of laughter were left. Lonergan reached the front porch and saw the man jump backward and duck into the thicker darkness opposite him. Lonergan ran across the street.

He reached the lawn but could see nothing but deep shadows between the houses and the empty blackness of the yards.

He shifted his direction toward the intersection. He'd fight them out here away from the women; he'd be damned if he'd reveal any worry because of a lookout. The pattern was familiar to him. It didn't matter whether gunmen came into the open quietly or rode down the middle of a street for everyone to see. They made certain it was known they were waiting—watching, one way or another—until their intended victim started to think and worry. Gunfights were won that way, once fear and doubt controlled a man.

Kling was on the saloon porch with Dave and Sid Jellison. The trio stood above the main crowd of men, who were arguing, jostling, bunched together in the street beyond the steps, packed in tight around some riders and four wagons and buggies. A gun slammed; glass shattered in one of the buildings. More glass crashed at the general store and the barber shop. Dave had waved to someone in the mob. A horseman pushed his mount free of the crowd and turned the big mustang toward the intersection.

Lonergan couldn't make out Dave's features or the other watching faces. The talk would start with this rider coming at him. They'd depend on the act, and the fear and worry the talk would bring.

The cowhand bore down on him, riding hard and wild, firing his gun into the air. Lonergan held out his own weapon and pointed it for the man to see. He kept on the roll of the lawn to make the rider cross the walk to get to him; and he continued his slow stride toward the trampling hoofs.

CHAPTER FIFTEEN

'Watch him!' a man called. 'He'll run you down!'

'Get up on our porch! Hurry, he'll ride right over you!'

Their voices echoed along the street and blended into the rising noise of the mob and the loud confused thumps of the mustang's hoofs. Lonergan angled higher on the edge of the lawn, in plain view against the yellowish light of the porch lamp. McGuire was the rider. He was crouched over the saddle horn, firing his fifth and sixth bullets into the darkening air.

Lonergan stood straight and tall, his Colt leveled. 'Swing him,' he shouted. 'Swing him away!'

A wild drunken, '*Yip-yip-yippee! Yahoo*!' came from the rider.

'Swing him! Turn that horse!'

McGuire snapped the trigger and hammer against the empty chamber and waved the weapon crazily while he pulled his mount left and diagonally across the street for the nearest porch.

Women screamed, children cried, scrambling for the open doorway of the house. The mustang's hoofs clomped loud on the wooden steps, the iron shoes chopping like hammer blows. Animal and rider reached the porch boards as the door swung in and slammed. All along the residential section, doors banged shut. Families doused porch lamps and watched through parlor and front room windows, fearful that the cowhand might charge their homes and do damage.

Lonergan shot a glance back at the rider, who was going off the porch and heading out along Cross. He holstered the .44 and held his open palm against his gunbelt. He couldn't see the entire center of the business district, but just the part of the mob that surrounded the buggies, and a surrey between the saloon and the Goodland Hotel. Night came fast; pinpoints of stars blinked in the blue-black sky. Dust was kicked up under the boots of milling cattlehands and men. The talk and shouting seemed like one continuous argument. Sheriff Loomis was in the middle of the gathering, while both of his deputies were at the outer edges trying to hold the wildness. Broken glass was everywhere; it littered the walks and the storefronts, the splintered pieces reflecting the light of the street lamps.

Lonergan worked his way around the edge and saw that Loomis was having trouble speaking to the drivers of the vehicles. Kling hadn't moved on the porch steps, nor had Dave or Sid. Kling had spotted Lonergan. He acted as if he hadn't, and he cupped both hands to his mouth and yelled with the rest.

'Let them go, Dobie. One more time. Your rig won't get hurt.'

The man in the seat of the largest vehicle, an expensive, fringe-topped surrey with two matched bays, shook his braided whip.

'One more race,' he told Dobie. The saloon owner had pulled himself onto the step plate and tried to make the cowhand get off. The driver shoved his free hand into Dobie's chest. 'I'll watch it. I didn't turn over before.'

'You almost did,' Dobie begged. 'No more races, please. Come inside. I'll set up.' He glanced across his shoulder at the angry, snapping voices. 'All of you, I'll set up.'

'No, we're gonna race.' The driver shoved hard and Dobie floundered back into the crowd. Lowney, alongside one of the buggies, grabbed Dobie's arm and pulled him onto the walk. The mob began to break when the whips cracked and the horses went into motion.

Dave Jellison called above the din of voices, 'McGuire's waitin' at the end of Cross. He's set up a startin' line. Winner gets a bottle! Two bottles! I'll split with Dobie!'

'I'll make the finish line,' Chingo Hobb yelled. He moved off the porch steps and waved at two cowhands to follow him. 'We'll light it up so's you can see!'

Laughter, shouts, and obscene curses were loud and uncontrolled. The mob surged back on both sides, the outer line bulging where they'd opened to allow the wagons to pull free. Three vehicles swung wide across the intersection. Wheels creaked while strained axles ground at the pull of the whipped horses.

Judge Roddy at the far side of the crowd worked with Loomis and the two deputies, all four trying hopelessly to control the shoving and pushing.

Lonergan reached the judge. The old man's bearded head shook. 'I don't know what they intend,' he was saying.'They've got to be stopped. Ernie, you can see that.'

'They're quietin', Judge. They'll calm down.'

'When? You tell me when!' He scanned the close buildings, motioned at the smashed glass and the silent figures of the store owners who watched from darkened interiors. 'They know now. They'll be with you.'

Lonergan said, 'You have Greeners in your office, Sheriff. You come out with shotguns, they'll see you mean it.'

Dobie spoke quickly, 'They'll go back inside after the race. I'll keep them in my place.'

'Look at those stores,' the judge said. 'That's just the start.'

'We told you we'd stand for that.' Dobie nodded vigorously with Lowney.

A cowhand took hold of Dobie's right shoulder and elbowed his way into the group. 'I want another bet! Same stakes as before!'

'I'll take a bottle, too,' another shouted. 'The buckboard loses, I pay double. Okay,

Dobie?'

'Sure. Sure,' the saloon owner agreed. 'Same as in the first race.'

'You're going to allow this?' the judge said to Loomis. 'You should be in charge. Anything that goes on should be under the law.'

'I'm out here,' the lawman answered. 'You tell me how I'm going to sit on everything with only two deputies.' He looked at the judge. 'I asked the Council for more money.'

'You can deputize Lonergan. He won't ask any money.'

Lowney, pressed in close to them by the shoving, jostling mob, interrupted. 'That'd be the worse thing to do. They'll calm down. You put a badge on Lonergan and they'll be out in this street with guns all night.'

'The Council won't agree,' Dobie said. 'We stood it so far and it'll change. We don't want nothin' from Lonergan.'

Chet Kling called from the porch, 'Sheriff, you'd better move them back or they'll get run down. Those horses'll ride right on them.'

Loomis flicked his stare back and forth over the heads and hats. The town men who were present watched from the porches and walks. Most of the cowhands were lined safely clear of mid-road, but here and there a small knot of drunks curved off the planks and bellied

182

wide into the street.

'Move back,' Loomis called. 'Get back in there.'

Lonergan looked up at Kling, his eyes as much on the Jellisons. 'You could call this whole thing off. One word from you and nothing happens.'

Kling shook his head. 'They're paid now. I can't stop a thing.'

'You can stop everything. Out in this street. In any part of this town, and you know it.'

Lonergan clipped his words short and moved up onto the edge of the walk, his eyes on Kling, Dave, and Sid. He'd chance the third Jellison joining a fight. Lew wasn't either of the two men he could see inside the saloon at the bar.

Kling smiled lazily. His glance wandered along the bunched faces, and he judged their reactions. Lonergan kept his stare on the three and waited. 'You've pushed this, Kling, you Jellisons,' he finally said. 'You know what you've wanted all along.'

'Dammit, he's the one doin' the pushin',' Dobie said. 'You can see that, Ernie.'

'Yes, Ernie, he tried it out back of my hotel, too. Alfred'll tell you that.'

Kling's grin widened. 'You don't move, you'll be run down, Lonergan.' He nodded past the sheriff and Judge Roddy to the west

183

end. A sudden glare of light flashed at the bandstand. Chingo Hobb and the cowhands had heaped dead branches in the center of the platform. Chingo hurled a lamp he'd taken from a porch into the pile. The blaze leaped into the air and brightened the entire length of the town.

Loomis shifted on the soles of his boots and switched his eyes from the fire to Lonergan. 'That's enough,' he said. 'This is big enough to handle.'

'Deputize more men, Sheriff. They should cover the homes and families.'

'Don't tell me what to do. Get back and stop tryin' to force a fight.' Loomis studied the bandstand. The platform had caught. Sparks and flame burst up as another thrown lamp smashed and splattered oil. 'I said get back.'

Lonergan watched Kling and the Jellisons. The trio looked away from him, their faces intent, their full attention toward the long side street where the out-of-sight buggies, surrey, and buckboard lined up on the darkened flat.

'They'll be headin' in,' a deputy said. 'Come on, you people. Move back.' He placed a hand on Lonergan's shoulder to force him higher onto the saloon walk.

Lonergan shook off the fingers and turned to retrace his steps. He paid no attention to

184

the remarks close by, or the shouted jeers. He was alone now, cut off from everyone. There would be no help from any quarter. The sheriff and his deputies were caught up with so much to cover, and the judge was standing mute and alone since he'd tried to bring a showdown.

Turning his head slightly, Lonergan's cold, gray eyes picked out the third Jellison on the porch now with the other two. The three and Kling watched only him, and he knew they'd come.

★   ★   ★

Dave Jellison said, 'Slow, Sid, take your time.'

'We've waited too long, dammit. He's goin' back to the Hollis place. Lew saw both them women in there.'

'They won't run. They can't do anything but stay.' He'd paused with one hand on the batwings. Cross Street was just beginning to lighten at the first sign of the moon. He could still make out Lonergan's figure beyond the intersection, and the big man's straight, sure walk. The sheriff, the judge, and the two deputies were lost in the cluster of sombreros and high crowned, wide-brimmed hats as they tried to hold the mob.

185

Dave nudged Chet Kling. 'Keep it goin',' he said. 'Once the wagons start down that road.'

'I will. I'll tell Chingo and I'll get down there.'

'Dammit, Dave,' said Sid. 'Lew's got the horses waitin'.'

Dave still held the swinging door so his brother wouldn't be able to shove through. There were no holes in his plan. Lonergan would stay out to cover the women. The law would be so busy once the race ended, with Chingo keeping the fire going. Dave visualized the Hollis yard mentally and moved Chet Kling and his brothers into place like a poker player setting up a pat hand. His face was wooden; his eyes narrowed in concentration. At last he nodded.

He motioned to Sid, pulled open the door, and said to Kling, 'Make sure they're tearin' up. No one gets hurt. Just keep the law damn busy.'

Sid had halted inside the saloon, blocked by Ike Hunt and J.P. Delock. The two cowhands staggered under the weight of the huge gilt-edged mirror. A cleaned and oiled Greener shotgun lay flat on the shiny glass.

Hunt's bearded face grinned widely. 'Dobie wouldn't sell,' he said. His feet were unsteady and he tottered as if he might fall. 'We're takin' it an' the scatgun he kept 'hind the counter.'

'You crazy?' Sid began. He glanced at Lew, who was waiting at the rear storeroom door. 'You'll have everyone in here.'

'He wouldn't sell,' J.P. Delock repeated. He was a small, wiry rider, whose eyes tended to bulge when he'd had too much to drink. They bulged now and watched Lew. Delock was ready to battle for the prize if he had to. 'We're takin' it. Don't you try to stop us.'

Dave laughed. He picked the shotgun off the mirror and shoved the swinging doors open for Ike to move his end through.

'This gun gets put back,' he said. 'Go down the side steps. Use the mounts close to the fire. You'll see better, and Dobie won't look that way.'

'Good man.' Ike guffawed, his words and laugh barely understandable. 'You'll get a piece, Dave. We're gonna sell it, see.'

'Get movin' so Dobie won't catch you.' Dave hung back another long second until the pair were on the porch with their burden and staggering toward the top step.

Sid pressed close to the half-frosted window and stared past the intersection into Cross, listening for the sound of the racing wagons rolling toward the center. 'Those two damned fools,' he said. 'They could have had Dobie and the law comin' inside.'

'They've helped us,' said Dave as he balanced the shotgun in his right hand and headed for the door Lew held open. 'They'll be more trouble for the law to straighten out. Gives us extra time. We can't miss, usin' this on both them women and Lonergan.'

CHAPTER SIXTEEN

The moon moved up, paling as it climbed. Lonergan continued his fast pace until he reached the Hollis lawn. Talk and obscene swearing went on at the far end of Cross. A wheel of a buggy had evidently become locked with a wheel on the buckboard, and the men were having a hard time untangling the iron rims. Dim shafts of yellowish light showed behind drawn shades and locked shutters, along with the occasional sound of a voice. Even the side windows usually kept open to catch the freshness of the Platte's breeze were closed. The people knew that more shooting would come, just as they knew that a stray bullet could kill innocent bystanders. A front window of the home beyond Janet's gleamed a streak of light as someone peeked out at him. Then the shade dropped into place and the house blackened again.

He could picture the uncomfortable closeness of the room and could feel the tenseness and fear in the air. It was as real as the mingled smell of the dry dust and the river dampness. He moved into the shadow of the porch, then glanced momentarily at the center of town. The mob had grown impatient; yells were called toward the wagons, and the moving mass of bodies was outlined against the high leaping, orange-yellow flame of the bonfire.

A crack of a whip exploded on the prairie like a pistol shot. Wagons and animals were blurred emerging shapes, as yet colorless and gray-dark in the growing moonlight. Horses whinnied, men cursed with the whipcracks, and the wheels began to roll.

Lonergan edged deeper into the shadows. The surrey appeared first, half a length in the lead, its iron rims churning, bouncing, throwing funnels of dirt and dust up at the buggies and the buckboard close behind it. Drivers hunched over in their seats and slashed their whips across the horses' flanks, bellowing for them to gallop harder.

The creaking, squeaking confusion of the vehicles thundered past the houses; the noise echoed between the homes, through the yards, and out onto the flat.

Lonergan strained his ears. A sound around the side of the house separated from the noise of the roadway.

He was moving, bent low and hugging the depth of the shadows, his Colt cocked and aimed into the deeper, thicker blackness of the yard to catch the sound again and spot where he'd place his first shot.

He halted at the end of the house, his body flattened against the clapboards. Then he stepped into the open. He heard only the rattle and rumble of the racing vehicles going past and the shouts that grew louder and louder.

Then a low scraping noise came at the front of the barn near the door. Lonergan crouched lower and slid around the corner. He stopped when he saw the dog.

The big, shaggy Collie was at the rubbish box trying to force off the lid. The noise of the street hadn't bothered it. When it sensed Lonergan, it jerked its head around, looked toward the adjoining yard, and scrambled away into the darkness. Lonergan's mouth was dry and his heart thumped. He took a deep, long breath, and let his trigger finger relax.

Shots banged in the center; the yelling raised to an uncontrollable fever pitch. He'd used too much time getting back here. He'd moved as quietly as possible, but the dog had still heard him. He'd have to find a better spot. The barn roof had taken on a whiteness under the climbing moon. The small side corral was a crooked bony line; rough-cut poles ran in and out between the posts. The outhouses and barns rose up behind the homes, formless but making individual shapes as the land lightened. Each building held a threat; every structure was a dark place for someone to hide.

A low tapping sounded behind him, more of a scratching of a nail on glass.

Janet Duncan was in the window looking down at him. Her white blouse was clear to him, and he saw the long barrel of the rifle she'd taken from above the fireplace. She pressed her forehead against the glass pane and said something he couldn't hear.

Lonergan waved her off, telling her to pull back behind cover and stay there. He moved while the shade fell into place, stepped past the house corner, across the sandy lawn that divided the yards, and stopped with his spine pressed flush against the solid wall of the neighbor's home. He listened for a noise, any hint of close sound.

★　　　★　　　★

Chet Kling had broken his way to the east edge of the crowd, ready to leave once the spectators surged in toward the finish line. He waited for the instant the sheriff, the judge, and the deputies would be caught up in the human flow of bodies.

Kling shut his mind to the noise and confusion and the gunblasts that pounded into the sky. He saw the sweating face of the lead driver, whose skin was reddish in the leaping firelight. His mouth was open wide while he yelled at his horse, his right arm flashing up and down with the whip. The buckboard at the left, in line with the two buggies, was on two wheels as it began the turn through the intersection; it threatened to tip or churn off into the onlookers. As one person, the crowd fell away. Those at the front threw themselves excitedly against the ones behind; the bigger heavier men shoved others aside, trampling the women and the smaller watchers. The wagon hung on its rims a frozen moment, and it seemed as if it would go over. The driver used his weight, shifted to the opposite corner of the seat, and the vehicle slammed down onto all fours and rolled ahead.

Again the watchers bulged out like a curved wave. Hats and heads and bodies were daylight clear in the bright, crimson-yellow flame. Chingo and the men with him fed the blazing fury with shutters, empty whiskey barrels, fence rails, and anything they could rip from a building or a nearby home. Now, as the wagons completed the wide turn past the main body of onlookers, they hurled the wood they had in hand and headed for the safety of the walks.

Two horses had backed from the rails into the roadway between the saloon and the flames. The riders, Ike Hunt and J. P. Delock, balanced something between them. It was the backbar mirror from the Drovers. Dobie saw them and ran out calling to them.

Gunshots ceased. The wild screams and yells lessened, then died to a quiet. Only the rolling of the wagons, the bouncing, jostling, clomping of hoofs, and the shouts of the drivers, who tried desperately to turn or slow before they were on the horses and men, could be heard.

J. P. Delock swung full in the saddle and let go of the mirror. He spurred his mount toward the mouth of the closest alleyway at the same instant as Ike Hunt. Dobie made a grab for the glass. Catching one end he tried to balance it; he held the gilt-edged corner like a juggler in a side show. But the weight was too much for him. The mirror tipped, yet he continued his attempt to drag it onto the walk.

The surrey made a crazy churning try to

turn but, pressed on by the vehicles behind that hadn't lost momentum, the driver kept his horse going ahead. A curdling scream came from Dobie's lips as he dropped the mirror and threw both arms over his face. Then his shout was lost in the thunder of the driving hoofs and the crash and cracking of splintering glass as horses and wagon wheels pounded over him.

Iron rims screeched and strained, and brakes gripped. A woman screamed; men shouted for control and quiet and ran into the roadway. Sheriff Loomis was in front of the suddenly silent crowd that moved closer and closer to the area lit by the fire.

Kling had believed he'd already heard the outbreak of the Jellisons' gunfire. He slowed his walk until he was sure the judge and the deputies were in the middle of the converging groups trying to help Loomis hold them down.

Kling quickened his stride, staring around until he could no longer see the lawmen. Every face was on Dobie's crushed body in the roadway; none as much as threw a glance toward Kling.

Kling whipped out his sixgun and increased his pace at each step. He crossed the intersection and broke into a run up onto the walk to use the homes for cover the closer he moved to the Hollis house.

★   ★   ★

In the silence of the houses and the back
yards, Dobie's terrified scream had come as a
shock that forced Lonergan into motion. The
crash had been a sudden loud thud; the
noises, confused as the wagons smashed wood
and glass.

He slowed before he reached the front
porch. The moon threw a floodlight whiteness
onto the roadway; its silverish light defined
the chimneys and the peaks of the buildings
and gave a shine to the slate roofs. The crowd
was a mass of dark, shifting, packed-tight
figures against the jumping flame. The
wagons, all bunched together, looked as if
they'd been stopped before the finish line.
Their drivers were standing in the seats
staring at the ground.

Lonergan had watched them only a few
seconds when he caught a flicker of movement
at the corner of the intersection. A man was
running toward the houses.

He threw himself sideward, intending to
use the Hollis porch and its rails and
supporting timber for cover until he was
certain who the man was.

Somewhere in the Hollis yard glass shattered. A woman's scream tore out of the rear of the house.

Silence came, a silence that was worse than the scream. Lonergan forgot the runner. His attention on the man had used long, precious moments. The first shot banged from within the house, the muffled yet unmistakable crack of a Winchester rifle. Then came the loud smashing of a kitchen window.

Two more shots exploded—one inside the house, one in the back yard. A man's voice shouted beyond the yard near the barn. Another answered, the words indistinguishable to Lonergan because of the loud boom of a shotgun striking solid wood and glass.

'Upstairs!' Lonergan yelled into the house. 'Get upstairs, Janet! Get up there!'

He was barely two strides from the corner; he slowed and crouched low before he turned into the yard so the attackers couldn't hit him as he came around. 'Run, Janet! Don't try to hold them! Get upstairs! Both of you. Get upstairs!'

CHAPTER SEVENTEEN

The shotgun boomed and the shot ripped into the corner of the house, shredding the clapboards and spraying splinters into Lonergan's face.

Janet's shrill yell tore out through the window. 'Two of them! Two at the back!'

'Upstairs! Get upstairs!' The rear door had been ripped wide open; only part of the bottom still hung on its hinge. He kept moving, not around the corner, but diagonally across the lawn into the deeper black shadows.

The gun that flashed on the porch drove a bullet through the exact spot he would have been in if he'd rounded the corner. The lead slug zinged behind him and whacked solidly into the side of the next house. A second flash spat from the same gun. Lonergan aimed, fired once, twice, then leaped clear of the house and threw a third shot at the shadowy figure near the shattered back door.

'Dave! Dave!' Sid Jellison yelled. He coughed and began to go down; his revolver triggered once more.

Lonergan felt the bullet strike and slice off the heel of his left boot. He tripped at the impact, hit the dirt, and sprawled flat. His hat flew from his head; pain ripped along his shoulder and leg as he slid on his chest and stomach.

The fall had saved him. Dave Jellison appeared in the rear doorway, a dark figure against the thicker blackness of the interior of the house. The shotgun belched yellowish-blue flame. The terrific roar of the weapon was like a dynamite explosion in Lonergan's eardrums.

Lonergan squeezed the trigger again and again, heard the swish of shot pass above him, and felt the heat of the blast sear his hair. His bullets used, he rolled toward midyard to gain the protection of the barn for a reload.

He stopped on the third roll. Not a sound nearby, but the third brother must be close. Dave was down and didn't make a motion. Lonergan pushed onto one knee and stood. The fingers of his left hand plucked cartridges from his gunbelt. Three quick limping strides and he was on the porch.

Sid lay on his side as if he slept. Blood showed on his shoulder and arm and ran down his forehead and cheek and mustache from the hole high on his head.

Dave had dropped facedown in the doorway. The top half of his body was on the porch stoop; the bottom half, still inside the tiny hallway. Lonergan had the Colt open.

The bullets were in his hand, ready to be shoved into the cylinder. The clomp of running boots at the far side of the barn was as loud to him as the footfalls behind him in the kitchen.

'Matt,' Janet called. 'They left horses waiting on the flat!'

'Stay in. Keep in there!'

He'd slapped the cylinder shut and had shoved the half-loaded sixgun into the holster. Crouched low, he gripped Dave Jellison's shoulder and threw the body onto its back. He straightened with the double-barreled shotgun in his hands. Then he broke the heavy weapon, felt inside the chamber. One cartridge still loaded.

The dark figure of a man rounded the barn corner and charged in fast. 'Dave?' Lew Jellison shouted toward the porch. 'Dave? Sid?'

'Hold it. Stop right there,' Lonergan told him.

Lew Jellison snarled out an obscene oath and fired. Lonergan squeezed the trigger, then ducked aside as Jellison's bullet thunked viciously into the door post. Lew was stopped in mid-stride, took the whole impact of the blast, and was smashed back and down like a wind-felled tree.

Lonergan moved out to the porch steps.

Shouts came from the center of town. Streams of lamplight slanted in square blocks through the windows of both neighboring houses. Lew was dead where he'd struck the ground, judging from the way his shirtfront was punctured. A match flicked and touched a wick in the kitchen. Janet carried the lamp into the hallway, halted on the threshold, and stared at Dave Jellison. Kate Morrow cowered in the doorway behind her.

'He broke into the kitchen,' Janet said. She grimaced as she looked from the dead man to Lonergan. 'I didn't know what to do when the door blew in.'

'There's more of them. Stay inside.'

'Come in with us. The sheriff has deputies. He can swear . . .'

'Keep in. Go upstairs if they get by me.'

He swung around to face the thump of running boots on both side lawns. Talk was loud and confused, and it grew rougher as the men converged on the yard. More oil lamps had been lit in the adjoining homes; the glare from the rear porches gave added visibility between the house and barn.

'Matt, please. We can all stay.'

'Don't come out here, Janet. No matter what happens, don't either of you step outside.'

He leaned over and gripped Dave Jellison

under the armpits. Half-lifting, half-pulling, he moved the body into the center of the porch and lowered it beside Sid. Dave's square face had a strangely shocked expression to it. The mouth was partly open; the teeth, shining white in the lamplight. Lonergan ran his hand across the lips and closed them. He straightened with the shotgun balanced flat against his hip.

One of Loomis' deputies was the first man to appear from the left corner; the carbine he carried was cocked and aimed. He slid to a halt at Lew's body. He stood as if unbelieving and looked from the shredded shirt front and chest to the other two dead men and Lonergan on the porch. Kling and four cowhands appeared behind him, and four more circled in from the right. They didn't have the open, dumbfounded stares. One quick gaze at the ground and they swung in a group to form a line beyond the steps. Any trace of drunkeness had vanished. Bunched in close, hands lowered carefully toward their gunbelts, they bumped arms and shoulders.

'Spread out,' Kling shouted. 'Spread the target.'

Lonergan limped onto the top step. 'Get a good look, Kling,' he warned. 'See what this Greener does.'

He was aware of men still circling behind

the ten. Faces were lost to him; only the fact that the mob grew and widened registered, and the knowledge that they could push right over him.

'You first, Kling,' he said in a quiet voice. 'You get the first barrel.' His eyes flicked left and right. 'Anyone else fool enough takes the second shell.' His tone hardened. 'Look at Lew Jellison. He got that tryin' to kill those women. You want that, come on! Come on!'

Dead silence fell. Judge Roddy and Sheriff Loomis had shoved through to the front of the line. Both brandished the hand guns they held as though they clearly intended to use them. Loomis' second deputy moved in alongside the first. The Winchester he aimed trembled in his hands. He pressed the stock against his side, firmly into the bone and flesh and it didn't shift a fraction of an inch.

Judge Roddy said, 'Step back. Don't touch your guns and step back.'

'Yes,' Ernie Loomis repeated. 'Back. Don't try to draw.'

Kling's hand, still poised above the ivory handle of his Starr .45, didn't lower. He motioned to Chingo Hobb and the others with his left. 'We c'n do it. There's twenty of us. More. We've got more.'

'One flick of that hand,' said Lonergan, 'you go, Kling.'

None of the other cowhands had tried to raise a finger. Lonergan eyed Chingo Hobb and McGuire, then let his glance slide across the semicircle of faces. 'Slow now, all of you. Unbuckle those gunbelts. Let them drop.' The Greener lifted inches to face level.

'Unbuckle and drop, I said. Hands only on the buckle.'

The puncher next to Kling moved his hand toward the center of his gunbelt.

'Don't, Teeter,' said Kling. 'We can . . .'

'Damn you, Kling,' the cowhand snarled. 'I got a wife and kids. I ain't part of this.'

'Me neither,' said a second. He'd flipped the buckle open to let the heavy holster slip down his leg to the ground. A third, then a fourth gunbelt dropped, and one by one the other cowhands unbuckled and backed away from their weapons. Chingo and McGuire were the last to hold position with Kling. Lonergan waved the double barrels at them, and McGuire unhooked and let drop.

Kling shot a quick, hate-filled glare to his left. 'Damn you, Mac.'

'I wasn't with them,' said McGuire, his eyes on the dead men. 'The Jellisons did the killin'.' He watched Chingo undo his buckle and allow the heavy Colt to fall to the dirt.

'Well, pick them up,' Judge Roddy snapped at the deputies. He stepped into the clearing with the two younger men, leaned low, and took the first gunbelt. Lonergan went down another step, then another. He set the damaged heel carefully on the wood in order not to trip. On the bottom stair, the shotgun barrels were ten feet from Kling.

'Take his gun,' he said to Loomis. 'He stuck so close to those three. He'd be in on the beatings. Ernie, you run this town.'

Kling shied away, and made the sheriff reach out to yank the sixgun clear of leather. Kling threw hasty glances around him at the other cowhands, then shook his head. 'Listen,' he said to Lonergan, 'I didn't touch Hollis.'

'You know who did.'

'No, I don't.' Loomis and his deputies were alongside Judge Roddy, all with arms weighed down by the cartridge-lined straps and holsters and weapons. Kling edged clear of them, his eyes on the twin muzzles of the shotgun barrels. 'Dave went to talk to him. He caught Hollis harnessin' up to leave. I didn't know he'd hurt him so bad.'

Lonergan shoved him toward the sheriff and Judge Roddy. 'Tell them. You must've known they were coming here.'

'I'll set up charges,' the judge said. 'Ernie, you heard Lonergan.'

At the rear of the crowd, the women who'd

204

been watching—neighbors of Janet Duncan and a few of the saloon women—began to break away and leave. Kling stared sullenly at the ground while Loomis and his deputies opened a path through the crowd. The judge faced the cowhands. 'You'll get your guns when you ride out.' He motioned to where Lowney, Fullerton, and Dexter stood silently together near the lawn. 'You can do any business you want, as long as it's quiet.'

He turned to Lonergan, aware that the cowhands were moving off behind the women. Lonergan followed part way along the lawn until he could see the intersection. He was watching for a disgruntled puncher to say or do something. One or two slowed momentarily to stare at the dead men. But they did not speak to each other or make even the softest side remarks.

'I'll run through the inquest,' the judge said. 'If you want to get out to your herd.'

Lonergan nodded. He leaned the shotgun stock-down against the side of the porch. 'You'll handle everything here.'

'I will. It'll be different when you bring in your beef.' He gestured at Kate Morrow, who was coming down the cement steps alongside Janet Duncan. 'With Dobie dead, you'll be leaving. Every one of you women.'

Lonergan saw Kate's nod. 'There'll be a

place to make a new start,' the judge added.

Kate smiled. The bruised cheek and side of her mouth were as stiff and tight as her lips.

Lonergan watched Kate walk away after the other people. He knew Janet was close to him. He could tell that the men and women talked while they returned to their homes, but he couldn't hear the voices clearly enough to understand a word. A window went up in the next house. The grating of a shutter being opened to welcome the night wind sounded, and that was enough. Reaction hadn't clouded any of his thoughts. He had no heart-pumping exhilaration within him, just the intense satisfaction that the people could relax now, and their children would never have a night like this again. He turned to Janet.

'Your leg wasn't hit?' she asked.

'No. There's enough of the heel to keep me going.' She watched him gravely, her small serious face questioning him. 'It's still early,' he went on. 'You'll want Lonnie home now. I'll ride out for you.'

'I do. I want to go with you.' She touched his hand, then she looked away toward the intersection of Cross and Frontier.

The banging that had come from the direction of the Drovers Bar had changed to a screeching of cloth tearing; the noise was loud in the night quiet. Lonergan took a step, then

206

paused.

One of the deputies crossed the roadway and shouted to Ernie Loomis. 'You okay, Sheriff?'

'Yes. You get back and take care of the office,' the lawman answered. He rolled what was left of the torn sign, THE TOWN IS YOURS!, into a round ball. Then he tucked it under his arm and continued on toward the long white length of cloth hanging from the town hall.

Lonergan smiled to himself, then to Janet Duncan. 'I'll hitch the buggy,' he told her. 'You can show me the way.'

Photoset, printed and bound in Great Britain by
REDWOOD BURN LIMITED, Trowbridge, Wiltshire